DOCTOR·WHO

The Art of Destruction

DOCTOR·WHO

The Art of Destruction

BY STEPHEN COLE

BBC
BOOKS

2 3 4 5 6 7 8 9 10

BBC Books, an imprint of Ebury Publishing
20 Vauxhall Bridge Road,
London SW1V 2SA

BBC Books is part of the Penguin Random House group of companies whose
addresses can be found at global.penguinrandomhouse.com

Penguin
Random House
UK

Doctor Who is a BBC Wales production for BBC One.
Executive producers: Russell T Davies and Julie Gardner
Series producer: Phil Collinson

This edition published in 2015 by BBC Books, an imprint of Ebury Publishing.
First published in 2006 by BBC Books.

www.eburypublishing.co.uk

A CIP catalogue record for this book is available from the British Library

ISBN 9781849909877

Commissioning Editor: Stuart Cooper
Creative Director and Editor: Justin Richards
Cover design by Henry Steadman © BBC 2006

Printed and bound in Great Britain by Clays Ltd, St Ives PLC

Penguin Random House is committed to a sustainable future for our business,
our readers and our planet. This book is made from Forest Stewardship
Council® certified paper.

MIX
Paper from
responsible sources
FSC
www.fsc.org   FSC® C018179

For Tobey, when you're older

The darkness played tricks on you, down here. The red light of the torch barely lit the surroundings, and in the cold blackness pressing in beyond it was easy to imagine you could glimpse things moving. Not the bats, nestling high up in the cave roofs in their thousands, but silent, looming creatures, waiting patiently in the dark to get you.

Kanjuchi shivered, and was cross with himself for feeling afraid. He must have made a hundred trips beneath the volcano and all he had ever encountered were the bats, their slimy filth on the floor and Fynn's precious fungus, which grew in it. But then, the caves and tunnels stretched on for kilometres, and so far they had only farmed a few hundred metres west and barely touched the eastern network. Now, with the early tests showing good results, they were excavating deeper and deeper…

'Come on, Kanjuchi. Get a move on.'

Adiel's voice made him jump. He turned to look at her.

'I've got stuff I need to do tonight, OK?' She was short and sparky, with hair in dreadlocks and a smile that was warm like a child's.

No smiles today. She seemed on edge.

'Sorry,' he said. 'I was just… just…'

'It's OK. This place gives me the creeps too.' She patted him lightly on the shoulder. 'Let's just get on to the new chambers and check how the 'shrooms have taken.'

Kanjuchi nodded and quickened his step along the stone pathway through the centre of the fungus. The red light didn't disturb the wildlife or the 'shrooms, but it made everything that bit creepier. The cave narrowed and the ceiling sloped down, and soon he was leading the way into one of the connecting tunnels.

'I hadn't realised Fynn had gone so deep,' Adiel murmured.

'Take a two-week vacation and this is what happens,' Kanjuchi replied.

'Progress?'

'Desperation. Results aren't satisfying the sponsors.'

She scoffed. 'No kidding.'

'He's had to step up the programme.'

The tunnel snaked from side to side. Kanjuchi tried to keep looking at the ashen ground ahead of him. He hated the tunnels most, relics of the route taken by the seething lava as it drained underground thousands of years ago. Now, in the dull red light from his torch, the formations left behind seemed like hideous faces screaming in pain. Stalactites hung from the roof like scores of teeth, forcing you to crouch lower and lower as you made your way along. The air was stale and cold, and Kanjuchi longed to be back in the scorching African sunlight above ground.

'This is the first of the new chambers.'

Kanjuchi stood aside to let Adiel through first. The narrow opening was between two boulders; she, of course, slipped gracefully into the cave without touching the sides. Kanjuchi sucked in his paunch and squeezed through after her with embarrassing difficulty. Damn Fynn and his corner-cutting, and damn that junk about preserving natural habitats – there should be clear ways in and out of the farm chambers.

'Why does he insist on following this line of research?' Adiel murmured, shining her data-get on the large, fleshy arrowheads. The data-get beeped to signal its survey was complete. 'He's obsessed. But if he thinks –'

'What's that?' Kanjuchi's torch beam had caught on something on the walkway beyond the fungal field. 'It's sparkling!' He crossed closer to see a nugget of metal just lying in the middle of the walkway. 'Looks like... gold.'

'Come off it. How can it be?'

'I don't know, but...' He shone his torch beyond and gasped. 'Adiel, look, there's more of it here! The whole pathway's littered with the stuff. It's sort of glowing.'

'It can't be *real* gold,' she said, sounding uneasy. 'Let's settle this right now...'

But Kanjuchi wasn't listening. He stooped to pick up the nugget for a closer look. It was glowing like a coal in a furnace. Suddenly it flipped and rolled closer, as if propelled by some invisible force.

As if it was eager to be held.

Astounded, Kanjuchi snatched his hand away. But he wasn't fast enough.

The glowing blob somehow *stretched*, darted forwards like a snake, touched his fingertips. Sucked at them. He cried out in fear.

'What the hell…' Adiel took hold of his shoulders. 'Kanjuchi, what is that?'

'Help me!' he shouted, trying to shake the blob free. But it was clinging on, beginning to distort and flow over his fingers like thick glue.

'Stop playing around –'

Kanjuchi gasped as a hot, searing pain shot through his palm. It felt like his fingers had been bitten clean off. But there they were in the dim red light, gleaming, flexing and twitching as if with a life of their own. Mutely he held them up to show Adiel. She backed away, staring at him in horror.

'Oh, my God,' she croaked.

'It's eating my arm!' he screamed, staring terrified as the stuff kept flowing, over his wrist, up on to his forearm. Panicking, he brushed at it with his other hand – and the glowing, flickering metal began to devour that too. 'No!'

'I'll get help,' Adiel told him, slipping back through the narrow gap in the boulders.

He tried to follow her, but got wedged in the opening. 'Adiel, come back!' He turned sideways, tried to squeeze through. But now his red-gold arms were rising from his sides of their own accord, anchoring him against the cold, distorted rock, trapping him there.

Through the gap he could see Adiel fleeing away from him down the sinuous passage. Only his screams followed her.

Engines rasping like a giant's dying breaths, the TARDIS forced itself into existence in the middle of the crop field. It grew solid only slowly, as if exhausted by its long voyage through time and space. Finally, there it stood, improbable and serene under the baking sun – an old-fashioned police box, like a big, blue blot on reality.

But if the incredible craft seemed a little worn out, its owner was most definitely not. He sprang from the box with the grace of a gangly gazelle, eyes wide and dark, brown hair bouncing over his brow. He grinned at the sight of the tall, fleshy plants pressing all around, then shook one by the leaves as if introducing himself. He puffed out his cheeks. 'Flaming hot, isn't it? Quite literally. Sauna in the Sahara sort of hot.'

He struggled out of his brown pinstriped jacket and flung it through the open TARDIS doors – just as a slim girl with shoulder-length blonde hair came out. She dodged aside yet still caught the jacket with the casual air of one who spends most of their life ducking whatever fate might throw their way.

'Thanks for that, Doctor,' she said, smoothing out the fabric.

'Rose Tyler!' He gave her a crooked smile of

appreciation. 'You really are something special, aren't you? Help me save the universe every other day, make sure we never run out of milk – and even offer a quality clothes-care service!'

'Don't thank me till you hear how much I charge.' Rose smiled sweetly back and tossed his pinstripes on to the TARDIS floor. 'It's boiling out here.' She smoothed down her light blue T-shirt so that it covered the waistline of her short denim skirt. 'Where are we this time?'

'Not sure,' the Doctor admitted, rolling up his grey shirtsleeves. 'Lots of weird alien static about when we dropped out of space-time. Whole area's polluted. Clogged the sensors.'

'So this is a planet that sees a lot of space traffic, then?' She stepped out and looked round at the rows of towering crops, listening to the way they rustled in the warm wind. 'Seems quiet enough. These plants are weird, though. Kind of like fat corn.'

'Sort of,' the Doctor agreed, taking hold of a fleshy leaf and tearing it. A gloopy liquid oozed out. 'Allo, allo! Or rather, *Aloe barbadensis*. Aloe vera!'

'Don't call me Vera.'

'Ha, ha. Oh, but it's lovely stuff. Good old aloe vera. Good for the skin, and *great* for sunburn.' He glanced reproachfully at the blinding sun, smeared some of the ooze on the back of his neck and set off along the nearest line of crops. 'So, high-yield corn that also produces aloe vera, what does that tell you?'

Rose closed the TARDIS doors and hurried along

after him. 'That this planet sells magic seeds?'

'That here be humans – probably future humans. Or at least, future human plants. Could be a colony? Dunno, though.' He stopped and jumped up and down on the dry soil. 'Feels like Earth. Earthish, anyway. Thought we were in the neighbourhood…'

'But what about the alien pollution stuff?' Rose asked, sniffing the air. 'Has everyone got their own spaceship in this time?'

'Seems to me –'

'Don't move,' snapped a low, warning voice close by.

'As I was saying…' The Doctor held obligingly still as gun barrels pushed out from both sides of the foliage, and glanced ruefully at Rose. 'Seems to me we're in something nasty and smelly – but probably very good for the crops here.'

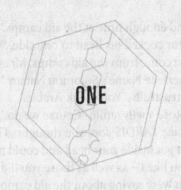

ONE

Rose had half-expected alien nasties to reveal themselves holding the high-tech rifles, so it was with relief that she saw they were very definitely human and probably as scared as she was. Two black men. One was in his thirties, wearing light khaki shorts and a sweat-stained shirt. The other was around her age and good-looking. He filled a muscle T-shirt quite successfully and wore a straw hat to keep the sun from his bare shoulders.

'How did you two get in here?' asked the older man.

The Doctor nodded cheerily to the plants waving around them. 'We often just crop up.'

'Answer me.'

'We found a gap in the… force field. No? Crack in the holo-shield? Wrinkle in the neutronic partition?'

'There was a hole in the fence,' Rose explained. 'But we didn't know we were trespassing. Where are we?'

'Like you don't know.' He looked at the younger man. 'Basel, do you recognise them?'

Basel sounded defensive. 'Why should I?'

15

'You spend enough time at the aid camps.'

The Doctor cocked his head to one side. 'Why should you think *we* come from the aid camps, Mr…'

'Chief Overseer. Name's Solomon Nabarr.' He eyed the Doctor mistrustfully. 'You speak Arabic.'

He gave Rose a wily smile. 'Course we do.'

Or rather, the TARDIS does, she thought. The ship was telepathic, it got inside your head and could translate any language you liked – as well as those you didn't.

'Now, you were saying about the aid camps…'

'Aw, come on, man. This is Chad –'

'Chad! Oh, fab! How cool is that? How *hot*, I mean. We're in Africa, Rose!'

'– and don't get me wrong but from the colour of your skin and speaking the language, you've got to be one of three things – aid worker, journo or activist.'

'Intelligent reasoning, like it.' The Doctor grinned. 'Completely wrong, though. Never mind. We're travellers, that's all. I'm the Doctor – not as in camp doctor, though some might say I have my moments – and this is Rose. You don't look very comfy holding that gun. Why don't you put it down and we can –'

Solomon wasn't to be put off. 'Only place you could stay without drawing attention is in a camp with the aid staff,' he maintained, 'unless you're being hidden by activists. So which is it?'

'They're not activists, Solomon,' Basel said, tightening his grip on the gun.

The Doctor looked at him enquiringly. 'How do you know?'

He shrugged. 'Activists wouldn't act so weird. I reckon they've escaped from somewhere.'

Escaping from here would be nice, thought Rose, who was busy angling her head to check out Basel's watch. It was a funky holographic digital thing, and obligingly told her it was 16.47 on 11 April 2118. She felt a familiar tingle of disbelief – to these blokes, her time was as dim and distant as the Victorians were to her. She wondered at all the things that must have changed since her own day.

But as the sound of screaming tore through the sweltering afternoon, she knew that some things would always stay the same.

Basel's head jerked sideways towards the screams. 'Sounds like Adiel.'

'Or like our cue,' said Rose, snatching away his rifle.

Solomon turned at the sudden movement and the Doctor disarmed him just as easily – before handing the weapon straight back with a brilliant smile. 'Shall we see if she's all right, then? Lovely! Come on…'

Shoving Basel's rifle back into his arms, Rose promptly took off after the Doctor and Solomon, crashing through the thick, waving stalks and leaves. As they broke the cover of the crop field Rose caught her first proper look at her surroundings. A huge mountain loomed like a thick shadow against the pristine blue of the sky. A futuristic building hugged the ground beneath it, all metal frames and dark windows. A stretch of red, desert landscape lay to her left, but right now she was running over bark chippings or something, and a short black woman in overalls that had seen better days was running frantically to meet them, some *Star Trek* tricorder-style gadget in her hand.

'Kanjuchi,' she panted as she all but fell into Solomon's arms. 'The tunnels... Something happened to him.'

Basel barged angrily past Rose to reach the girl. 'What happened to him, Adiel?'

'Where is he now?' asked Solomon urgently.

'New growth chamber, he was screaming. We found some weird gold stuff and it...' She pulled free from Solomon and buried her face in Basel's T-shirt. 'It *ate* him.'

'This sounds *right* up our street!' roared the Doctor with embarrassing enthusiasm.

Adiel didn't even seem to notice. 'He's stuck in the chamber, couldn't get out!'

'Rose, help Basel look after Adiel,' the Doctor instructed.

'Just quickly.' She took hold of his shirt collar and pulled him close towards her. 'It's 2118. Is that future-ish enough to explain that space pollution you picked up?'

'Nope,' he said simply. 'Right then, Solomon, show me the way to these tunnels.'

Solomon shook his head. 'You're staying here.'

'Stop wasting time! I'm not!'

He raised the gun. 'You *are*.'

'It's not even loaded!' the Doctor protested, grabbing it back off him and squeezing the trigger. Shots rang out, and Rose and Basel yelped as several stalks of aloe corn met the reaper early. The Doctor hastily chucked the rifle way into the crop field, out of reach. 'All right, then, it *is*

loaded. But aren't we wasting time? I think so. Now –
tunnels! Adiel was running in this direction, *ergo*…' He
started to run off towards the mountain.

'Come back!' roared Solomon, taking Basel's rifle and
chasing after the Doctor. 'Send some manuals to search
the fields,' he called back over his shoulder. 'Check this
pair haven't damaged the crop. They might have planted
something!'

'Like what,' Rose called after him. 'Magic beans?' She
shook her head as she watched the Doctor sprint away
through the shimmering heat haze, Solomon hard on his
heels, waving the gun. 'See ya, then.'

She looked at Basel. Not having a gun meant he could
put both arms around the shivering Adiel, and he had
wasted no time doing so. But his dark eyes were rooted
on Rose.

'I won't give you any trouble,' she promised him. 'But
maybe you should make her a cup of tea for the shock or
something, yeah?'

'Or something,' Basel murmured. He seemed to reach
a decision. 'All right. Come on. Help me get her inside.'

Solomon Nabarr pelted after the intruder, the stitch in
his side tugging hard with every step. 'Stop!' he shouted
for the tenth time. The Doctor was a good twenty metres
ahead of him, nearing the entrance to the underground
network now, and the gap was widening. Solomon fired
a warning shot into the air.

The Doctor skidded to a stop and turned indignantly.
'Look, Solomon, I'm not being rude – well, maybe I am –

but how about you get your priorities right? I reckon I might be able to help. If it turns out I can't, you can wave your gun about, chuck me out, all of that. Deal?' Not waiting for an answer and ignoring the raised gun, the Doctor jogged over to the steel doors gaping open in the rock. 'Through here, is it?'

Warily, Solomon nodded. 'All right. But you're going in ahead of me so I can keep my eye on you. I'll direct you.'

The doors gave on to an access tunnel. The temperature dropped sharply, which was welcome after the run. The lights were turned almost as low as the jagged roof above them, but slowly Solomon's eyes adjusted to the crimson glare.

'Lava tubes!' the Doctor declared, staring all around as he walked. 'Molten lava pours down the volcano, the outer layers cool and solidify, but the core stream continues to flow – and evacuates itself completely to leave behind empty tube-ways through the rock.'

'I did actually know how the tunnels come to be here,' said Solomon wryly, as they reached the first of the caves. He took two torches from their hooks on the wall and passed one to the Doctor.

'Blades, helictites… Geologist's dream, this little lot. How far does the network stretch?'

'Several kilometres, Fynn says.' As he hurried on through the enormous cavern, Solomon's shoe squelched in something wet and smelly. He grimaced and wished for protective clothing. 'We've only cleared a few hundred metres so far. The tubes are very fragile to the east. We're trying to shore them up but resources are limited…'

'What resources? Aha!' The bats rustled and chittered up above as the Doctor's exclamation echoed round the cave. 'I get it. You're farmers!'

'This is Agricultural Technology Unit 12.'

'Farmers farming fungus inside a volcano! Genetically modified, is it, like the crops?'

Solomon grunted, continuing onwards. 'The world needs food and there's precious little land left in which to grow it. Global warming, desertification…'

'So you're using your "agriculture technology" to grow grub in the less obvious places.' He considered. 'Yep, under a volcano, that's not at all obvious. And if we're in Chad, we must be walking about underneath Mount Tarsus, right?'

'You expect me to believe you don't even know –'

The Doctor skidded to a slithery stop on the slimy walkway. 'Hang on. Tarsus's still active, isn't it?'

Solomon didn't stop to wait for him. 'No eruptions for eighty years.'

'Then aren't you overdue one?'

'How'd you think the agri-board beat them down on the land price?' Solomon muttered. 'Come on. It's just through there.'

He gestured with the gun along the passage that led to the freshly excavated growth chamber. The Doctor rounded a turn in the passage – and came to a sharp halt.

'No tricks,' warned Solomon.

'Tell *him* that,' said the Doctor quietly, moving aside so

Solomon could come forwards.

He stared in disbelief, as if what he was seeing could be a trick of the red torchlight. Standing in front of the entrance, arms wide open, was what looked to be a golden statue. A statue of a man. The features were twisted and warped, but it was clearly –

'Kanjuchi,' Solomon whispered, feeling his stomach twist. He started forwards, but the Doctor took hold of his shoulder, held him back.

'No. Don't touch him.'

'But he's been hurt!'

'I'll examine him. I'm the Doctor, remember?' He advanced warily on the statue. 'Though even from this distance, I'd say he was dead.'

Solomon felt his legs sag beneath him, leaned against the rough basalt wall and tried not to be sick. 'Who would want to...' He shook his head. 'It's like he's been painted all over. Is that what killed him?'

'Like in James Bond, you mean? *Goldfinger*, that was the one.' He beamed over at Solomon. 'Who's playing Bond these days? Cal MacNannovitch was my favourite – it's always the one you grow up with, isn't it?' The Doctor's smile dropped. 'But no. Urban myth. People don't suffocate when you paint their skin. Something else killed this man.' He gingerly tapped Kanjuchi on the arm and a dull clang rang briefly round the tunnel. 'This stuff is way heavier than paint. It's holding him upright. And it's still warm. Suggests some sort of physical reaction is continuing.' He whipped out a pair of chunky spectacles from his pocket and hooked them on to his sharp, straight nose, then peered into Kanjuchi's open mouth. 'The stuff's in here too. Coating his tongue, the inside of his mouth, back of the throat…'

Solomon hardly knew what to say. 'How?' he croaked.

'Dunno. I'll have to take samples, run a full chemical analysis…' He straightened, looking at Solomon. 'Here's a funny thing, though. Didn't Adiel say she left him inside the chamber?'

'He… he must have struggled out.'

'I suppose he must have. But look at him.' The Doctor put away his glasses. 'Doesn't look like he was frozen mid-struggle, does he? He squeezed through that narrow exit and planted himself right in front of it – feet firm together, arms wide apart.'

'Trying to keep whatever did this to him in there,' Solomon reasoned. 'It must still be inside.'

'Yeah, he does look like he's standing guard, doesn't he?' The Doctor's face was pensive. 'I think we should have a quiet word with Adiel, find out exactly what happened in there.'

'Poor girl's only just back from holiday. She'll need another one to get over this.' Solomon rubbed the bridge of his nose. 'I must tell Fynn.'

'Who's this Fynn again?'

'Director of Development, in charge here. He'll contact Law Enforcement.'

'Oh, blimey. That's all we need. A band of butch soldiers with big guns and closed minds.'

'They'll find who did this,' Solomon murmured, but he was talking to himself more than the Doctor.

'Who? What d'you mean, "who"? You heard Adiel, some gold stuff ate him!' The Doctor frowned, lost in thought. 'Suppose I'd better have a word with him.'

'Who?'

'Your man Fynn, of course! Come on. D'you want to lead the way? No, tell you what, I'll go first again, shall I? You can keep pointing the gun at me. It might help you believe you've got some power over the situation...'

The Doctor stalked away and was soon lost in the crimson shadows of the winding tunnel. Solomon followed, aware of the sightless, glittering eyes of Kanjuchi on his back. Trying not to imagine the last things they had seen.

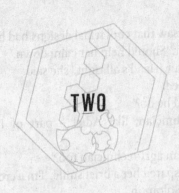

TWO

Rose had held Adiel's hand while Basel directed a couple of skinny farmhands to check out the crop fields, then he'd taken over and led them both into an empty common room. There was a TV screen no thicker than a fiver on one of the taupe walls, a shabby pool table, a tank of tropical fish and various bits of furniture that had seen better days. But at least the place was air-conditioned – a big relief after the stifling heat outside.

Adiel sat rigid on one of the threadbare sofas, staring into space; she looked an even bigger state than her stained overalls. Basel had prised the tricorder thing from her hands and now she fumbled idly with the beads on her necklace, which sparkled in the dusty sunlight coming through the large windows. Basel poured her a drink from the fridge. It smelt fruity and fresh, wonderful. Then he added a tablet, which fizzed the concoction up.

'Passive-pill,' he announced, chucking his hat on a

chair. Rose saw that cool tribal designs had been razored into his hair. 'Should help her calm down.'

'Hope your friend's all right,' she said.

He grunted.

'What did he do?'

'Agri-technician, like Adiel – part of Fynn's Food Squad.'

'Are you an agri-technician too?'

'Me?' He spared her a brief smile. 'I'm a crop inspector. I report to Solomon.'

'You inspect them, he oversees them, right?' She did her best to seem impressed. 'So, inspecting crops, that's got to be… um, fun.'

His smile grew a little in size and charm. 'It stinks.' He nodded to the fridge. 'You can grab a drink if you want.'

Her eyes met his. She looked away first, with a smile, and helped herself to a can.

'You saw the crops and got hungry, sneaked inside,' Basel ventured, slipping a comforting arm round Adiel's shoulders. 'Am I right?'

'You said it.' Rose took a big swig of her drink, silently toasting him for inventing her a cover story.

'Are you refugees, then? From the fighting?'

'You could say that,' Rose agreed. 'Seen a lot of fighting, me and the Doctor.'

'Boyfriend?'

'Best friend.'

'How bad is it in Moundou?'

'Um… bad.' She realised guiltily that her knowledge of Africa was pretty much non-existent. Poverty, war, disease… she knew it all went on from the news on TV, but didn't have a clue about the real issues. 'It's, like, *really* bad. We were glad to get away.'

'Yeah, the rehousing camps aren't fun. I do volunteer work at the one in Iniko when I'm off-shift. Hang at the school… you know.'

'Helping the kids and that?'

'I guess.' He looked awkward, defensive and proud all at once. 'Teachers give me lessons in return, see.'

'Huh! How ungrateful is that,' joked Rose – and straight away knew she had put her foot right in it.

Basel's eyes had hardened. 'How old d'you think I am?'

'Twenty, twenty-one? I dunno.'

'Yeah, well, I don't know either. Till last year I couldn't even count that far.' He turned up his nose. 'You know other languages and stuff. You learned loads at school, I bet. I don't even know when I was born. My dad died in the fighting, century's end. Mum was sick and never got better. I had to look after my brothers and then…' He turned back to Adiel, squeezed her shoulders as if she was the one who was hurting. 'Anyway. Never had much time for schooling. Only work, wherever I could find it.'

Rose rugby-tackled the change of subject. 'And here you are,' she said brightly. 'Nice little farm next to a mountain.'

'It's a volcano.'

'Seriously?' Rose had never seen a real volcano.

'And it's not a nice little farm either.'

So much for saving the conversation. She'd given him the right hump. 'Well… what is this place, then?'

'Just one more agri-unit sucking the land dry. Africa has debts it can never pay off, see? It rents out land to Europe and America for a handful of bucks so they can feed their people – while our own go on starving.'

Rose shifted in her seat uncomfortably. 'You're here, though, working for them.'

'I need money and this is the quickest way to earn it,' he said, a little more quietly. 'I've got to get out, get myself a proper education, get taken serious. Make people care about what's happening.' His arms slipped from round glassy-eyed Adiel as he leaned forwards, warming to his topic. 'Used to be just cotton and coffee and stuff Africa got ripped off for. Now the big corporations are taking native plants and animals, taking their genes apart, finding cures for diseases and stuff. They get rich, Westerners get better lives and we get next to nothing.'

'It's known as bio-piracy.'

Rose started at the sound of the cool, considered voice, saw a dignified-looking black man in a lab coat standing in the doorway. It was hard to tell how old he was – late forties maybe? His hair was greying but his skin was smooth and ebony-dark.

'However, Basel knows that although I direct the scientific research at this unit, I am just as opposed to the trend. I intend that my work will benefit the world, not only a portion of it.' The man looked at Rose, brown eyes wide and enquiring. 'My name is Edet Fynn. I wasn't expecting visitors.'

'I doubt you were expecting one of your agri-technicians to wind up gold-plated either,' said the

Doctor, charging into the room and making Fynn jump a mile. 'But these things happen.'

'He's the Doctor,' Rose offered apologetically. 'I'm Rose.'

'Here to help, like the Koala Brothers.' The Doctor forced his bum between Basel and Adiel as he plonked down on the sofa. 'She talking yet?'

'I gave her a p-pill,' said Basel. 'She's coming down.'

'What's going on?' Fynn turned in bewilderment to Overseer Solomon, who had shuffled quietly into the room, still holding his rifle. 'Where did these visitors come from? I had no –'

'Kanjuchi is dead, Director,' Solomon said.

Fynn stared. 'Dead?'

Basel shook his head. 'You're joking.'

'What happened?' asked Rose.

'That's the 24-carat question.' The Doctor waved a hand in front of Adiel's eyes. The girl didn't respond, her face a blank mask, fingers still turning her beads. 'Adiel, sweetheart, that's a lovely necklace. Where did you get it, hmm?'

Rose frowned, but Adiel actually responded. 'I made it,' she whispered.

The Doctor nodded encouragingly. 'Those stones are lovely.'

'They are local stones.'

'Not just stones, though, are they? I reckon they're tektites. Glassy crystals often formed as the result of a meteor impact. Or something from space anyway.' The Doctor looked over at Fynn. 'Got any craters round here?'

'No.' Fynn stepped forwards, disbelief boiling over into anger. 'But apparently I have a member of staff lying dead –'

'Standing up, actually.'

'– while you sit there discussing a necklace!'

Rose got up, raising her hands in a 'whoa there' gesture. 'He's trying to ease her back by talking about normal stuff, yeah?'

'Normal,' echoed Basel, his head in his hands.

'Hang on,' said the Doctor, 'what am I sitting on?' He reached behind him and produced the tricorder. 'Wow! A data-get… You still use these!'

Basel snatched it off him. 'It's Adiel's.'

In turn, Fynn took it from Basel. 'The data on the fungus crop I came for,' he said distantly, looking at the readout. 'No, wait… This isn't right…'

'Kanjuchi thought it was gold,' said Adiel. Her voice was quiet but it riveted the room. 'I wanted to prove he was crazy. I did a scan.'

Fynn looked at the Doctor. 'These readings are gibberish. The data-get's faulty.'

'Or else it's trying to break down chemical elements it's not programmed to recognise.' The Doctor half-smiled, but his eyes were dark and serious. 'Elements that aren't the product of Earth geology.'

Rose shut her eyes and waited for the inevitable storm of outrage and disbelief. But the room had fallen silent.

When she opened her eyes again she saw why.

A farm worker in dirty denim had pushed into the common room, his skin glistening with sweat. He was holding a golden bundle in his arms.

'Put it down, Nadif!' Solomon yelled beside him, as if the bundle was a bomb.

Clearly frightened, the worker obliged. His find hit the ground with a dull clang. Everyone stared – then Rose realised what she was looking at. It was a golden statue of a huge bird of prey – looked like an eagle in big gleaming knickerbockers.

Fynn stooped to see. 'Such craftsmanship. It's a work of art.'

'That's a vulture!' breathed Basel. 'A solid-gold vulture!'

'It's not gold,' the Doctor told him. 'And not a statue. That was a real vulture once. A living thing, enveloped in this same augmented magma.'

'What?' Fynn looked at him crossly. 'Augmented by whom?'

'I found it in the west field,' said Nadif fearfully. 'It was trying to fly, but it couldn't. It turned to… to *this*. Right as I watched.'

The Doctor shoved his hands in his pockets and nodded. 'Anything else?'

'That isn't enough?' Basel wondered.

Fynn cleared his throat. 'May I remind you, Doctor, that I am the Director here?'

'Then start directing!' He pointed down at the vulture. 'We've got to get on top of all this before *it* gets on top of us.'

Fynn turned to Solomon. 'All right. Organise your teams to search for any more affected wildlife.'

Solomon nodded gravely and left with Nadif.

'There must be another way into that cave,' the Doctor reasoned. 'Somewhere the wildlife's using.'

'Impossible,' said Fynn, looking edgy. 'The growth chamber has to be secure, no light, no change in temperature. The fungus can only thrive in a specific, controlled environment.'

'Looks like whatever else has turned up in that chamber's not so fussy,' said Rose.

'There was no daylight visible when Kanjuchi and I were inside,' Adiel offered.

'Two options,' snapped the Doctor, prodding the golden bird with his foot. 'Either the vulture found a hidden way into that chamber or else this happened to it somewhere else.'

Fynn crossed to the door. 'We must get over there and see for ourselves.'

'There we are, then! Only took half an hour.' The Doctor joined him in the doorway. 'Come on, Rose.'

'No, Doctor, your friend stays here. The crop is at a crucial stage and the less disruption in the growth chambers the better.' The look Fynn gave Rose was as cold as his tone. 'On the way over, perhaps you will explain to me precisely who you are and how you come to be here.'

'Perhaps,' agreed the Doctor. With a roll of his eyes at Rose, he hurried from the room.

'Stay with the girls, Basel,' Fynn called over his shoulder, rushing to catch up.

Rose eyed the metallic vulture. 'With the birds, you

mean.' She was thinking uneasily about that space pollution the Doctor had mentioned. That and the tektites around Adiel's neck – stones made by something falling from space in the local area. You didn't need a degree in weird stuff to figure out there was most likely a link here.

Adiel was staring at the golden statue too, her brown eyes glistening with the tease of tears. 'Why'd this have to happen?' she whispered. 'Why today?'

'Why any time?' said Basel gruffly.

'I can't believe Kanjuchi's dead,' she went on. 'If I hadn't run out on him, maybe –'

'Maybe you'd be dead too,' said Rose.

The tears dropped down her cheeks and her eyelids dropped with them as the p-pill took effect. 'Don't let me fall asleep. There're things… things I need to…' Adiel fell against the soft sofa cushions and started to snore gently.

'That golden thing gives me the creeps,' said Basel quietly.

'Me too,' Rose admitted. 'It's still so… sort of lifelike. I mean, I know it was alive, but it still looks like any second it's going to –'

The bird suddenly turned its bald, golden head and fixed her with molten eyes. Then it launched itself up from the floor, screeching and flapping its massive, gleaming wings, flying straight for her face.

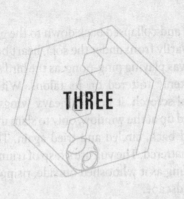

THREE

Rose dived aside with a shriek of alarm, bounced on the sofa cushion and tumbled off it on to the floor. She covered the back of her head with her hands – as if that was going to make Big Bird think twice about ripping into her with that sharp, shining beak...

Then suddenly something hard and heavy landed on top of her. It was Basel. 'What are you doing?' she gasped.

'Protecting you!' he said, as if this was somehow obvious.

The metal vulture's wings whistled through the air above them. 'Get off me, you muppet!' she hissed. 'We've got to get proper cover!'

'Under the couch,' said Basel, and they squirmed with some difficulty beneath it.

Rose looked at him. 'What about Adiel?'

'Threw a blanket on her.'

'Next time, I'll take the blanket and you can jump on her, yeah?'

There was a loud slam as the golden creature smashed

into a wall and collapsed back down to the ground. Rose watched warily from under the sofa, heart bouncing like her chest was playing ping-pong, as the bird struggled up and drunkenly tottered on its talons. With a grating, mechanical screech, it beat its heavy wings once more and flapped up at the window, only to slam into the glass. It bounced back, circled and tried again. This time the window shattered. The vulture's rasp of triumph was like gears sticking as it whooshed outside, rising up over the baking landscape.

Rose was first out from beneath the couch. 'There goes the air-conditioning,' she said, wincing as sandy grit blew in through the broken window. 'Come on. We can't let Big Bird just disappear.'

'Who?'

Basel pulled back Adiel's blanket, checking she was OK. It seemed that she'd slept through the whole thing.

'Never mind,' said Rose. 'Let's just get after it. It was stone dead one minute – well, *metal* dead – and then it came back to life! The Doctor is so gonna want to study it.'

'Let *him* catch it, then.' But almost immediately Basel seemed to have second thoughts. 'No, hang on. You're right. We *should* get after it.'

'Why the change of mind?'

His eyes widened. 'If the bird came back to life…'

Rose nodded. 'Maybe so's your mate Kanjuchi.'

Basel leaped through the jagged hole in the glass, Rose right behind him, kicking up sand and bark as they ran. High above, gliding through the glaring blue of the sky, was the weird vulture. Like them, it was making for the dark silhouette of the volcano.

Fynn crept reverently through his growth chambers, the data-get held tight in one hand. Usually he loved coming here, to the cool, quiet caves. It was like a return to childhood. The chitters and scuffles of the bats reminded him of the funny noises made by the air-con in his mother's Nigerian apartment. The warm red haze was like his old night-light.

The young Edet Fynn had spent night after night hatching plans and possibilities in his bedroom as to how he would transform the world of war and famine and death around him into one of new life. His mother was a scientist and his father had been too, but he would be greater than either.

Edet Fynn was going to save the world. And the things in these caves and passages would help him achieve that.

'Oops,' said the Doctor behind him, slipping in guano and almost losing his balance.

Fynn bit his lip and said nothing. The man had finally shown some ID that proclaimed him to be from the Global Farming Standards Commission, here to make a spot inspection of the agri-unit. A pain. Especially on a day like this one was shaping up to be. At the back of his mind lurked the suspicion that this was all some elaborate practical joke that the staff were in on. But he would play along for now. Let them have their fun. Give people what they want and they tend to go away quicker; that had always been his mother's advice. After what happened to his father, she never had time for anyone who –

'Blimey, this stuff's slippery,' said the Doctor, almost stumbling off the pathway.

'Be careful,' Fynn hissed. 'The fungus is very fragile.'

'How did you stumble on to it, anyway?'

'The bats' waste had built up here in the old lava tubes for hundreds of years. A natural fungus was growing on it.' He crept on through the cavern. 'One of the oldest, most primitive forms of life on Earth. Fungi do not require sunlight, do not need to produce chlorophyll as plants do. They feed on anything, dead or alive, breaking down matter and digesting it in order to grow.'

'*Almost* anything,' the Doctor agreed.

'I am evolving in my fungus a taste for many kinds of organic matter,' Fynn explained. 'I have already re-engineered its DNA to increase the nutritional value. I have enhanced its life cycle so that it grows tall and fleshy. If I can only make it hardy enough to withstand different environments – extremes of heat and cold... '

'Then it could be farmed where conventional crops never grow,' the Doctor concluded.

'The Earth's crust is up to fifty kilometres thick in some areas,' said Fynn. 'Imagine the potential crop yield if we were to farm one thousandth of it!' He smiled to himself. 'Imagine how my critics will eat their words.'

'Why, what have they been having a go about?'

He paused, steeled himself. 'The fungus is unfortunately poisonous.'

'Ah.' At least the Doctor didn't laugh, as so many

others had. 'That does sort of offset the nutritional value a bit, doesn't it?'

'It is simply a matter of finding the right medium in which to grow the fungus. I will achieve it. I have already performed experiments which would...' He saw the exaggerated innocence in the Doctor's expression and realised he was being patronised. 'Those who gainsay me are fools,' he said quietly, 'wishing to hold back human progress.'

'Let me guess – they see corn and aloe vera growing on the same stalk and they think Frankenstein, scary science, all that.'

'Genetic modification is more an art than a science,' Fynn insisted.

'So if the masses can't eat your mushrooms, they can gather round and admire them instead, right?' the Doctor said. 'Well, speaking of admiring, Kanjuchi is just through here. Remember him? The member of your staff who's dead?'

Fynn closed his eyes. This *had* to be a practical joke. The golden vulture, the faked readings on the data-get, it was all nonsense...

As they turned the corner of the sinuous passage, he was busy rebooting the sensors. And so he almost walked into Kanjuchi, gleaming like gold in the red haze, his face a metal mask, distorted with fear.

If it was a statue, it was incredibly lifelike.

'There you go. Now, that really *is* a work of art.'

Fynn stared at the Doctor. 'If you're trying to trick me...'

But the Doctor tapped the scan button on the data-get. A few moments later the diagnosis flashed at him in cool blue liquid crystal: ORGANIC-MINERAL CONTENT, COMPOSITION UNKNOWN.

'Kanjuchi has been affected – maybe even *infected* – by an alien substance.' The Doctor was looking at him sternly, as if daring him to disagree. 'I think it's something that's mixed with magma from the depths of this volcano and re-engineered it. Questions are – why, how, what and from where?' He smiled suddenly. 'Cheer up. At least we know *when*. Roughly speaking, anyway.'

'Doctor...' The screen on the data-get had started blinking and Fynn showed him.

COMPOSITION SHIFTING.

Suddenly a splitting, crackling sound exploded from the golden statue. Kanjuchi's already ample stomach seemed to swell larger. His head bobbed slowly from side to side as his neck bulged, as if fluid was pumping beneath the gilded skin. The perfectly sculpted clothes stretched and deformed as the shoulders broadened, the legs extended. It was like looking at the same statue reflected in a distorting mirror. Bigger. Bulkier. Still more disturbing.

'I think it's time I did a little composition-checking of my own,' the Doctor announced. He produced a small ceramic tool from his trouser pockets. The tip glowed blue as he held it against one of the figure's slab-like fingers.

Then suddenly the grotesque figure lashed out in a single savage movement. Its huge hand struck the Doctor in the chest, smashing him against the rough basalt wall.

Fynn cried out in shock and alarm. He held totally still, waiting for any sign that Kanjuchi might move again. But the figure remained immobile. Cautiously, Fynn crossed to where the Doctor lay in a bony heap. 'Are you all right?'

'What?' The Doctor's eyes snapped open. "S'OK, don't worry. I think I got my sample.' He undid the top buttons of his shirt and peered down at himself. 'Yeah, I can just pick the residue out of my ribs.'

With a drunken smile, the Doctor's head lolled back and his eyes shut, leaving Fynn alone with the hideous, bloated figure. Its eyes seemed fixed on him, not only reflecting the crimson light but absorbing it, burning with dark energy.

And as the shock and disbelief crowded in on his rational thoughts, the noises and the cool and the red glow signalled other childhood memories. They put him in mind of those long nights when the nightmares came, when he cried out for his dad, who was never coming back, and when the shadows pressed in all around like these dark, distorted walls.

Only down here the sun would never rise.

Fynn screwed up his eyes, trying to marshal his thoughts, to make sense of the impossible things he had witnessed.

When he opened them again, the burnished statue was standing a metre further to the left.

And the way into the chamber was clear.

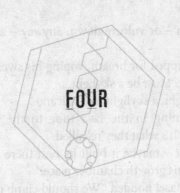

FOUR

Solomon watched as Nadif and a handful of the perimeter guards spread out through the crop fields, hunting for more golden creatures that only scientists could explain away.

While he wasn't a man of science, Solomon did know one thing.

'It's my fault,' he murmured aloud, wiping a trickle of sweat that the sun had no sway over from the back of his neck. *All my fault.*

And only I can do anything about it.

Steeling himself, he trudged off towards the sealed entrance of the eastern cave network.

The climate made running harder than Rose would have believed. The blazing sun was merciless, the air so hot it hurt to breathe. Gusts of warm wind blew sand in her eyes and she had to keep blinking them clear.

Even so, she saw the dazzling vulture swoop down on to a ledge in the foothills of the volcano. It seemed to duck down – or vulture down, anyway – and vanished from view.

Basel stopped for breath, wiping his sweaty forehead on his arm. 'Must be a skylight.'

'Yeah, right, a skylight in a volcano.'

'An opening in the lava tube to the surface,' he explained. 'It's what they're called.'

'So, what – maybe it built its nest there and found a way into this growth chamber place?'

'Right.' Basel nodded. 'We should climb up there and check it out.'

Rose dabbed at her dusty eyes and gauged the distance. It wasn't really so far up, but in this heat... 'What's got you so keen?'

He half-smiled. 'Maybe I just want to impress you.'

'Oh yeah?'

'Maybe.'

He was off again. Not to be outdone in the middle of some serious flirting, Rose forced herself to match his pace. They reached the rocky side of the volcano. A portakabin had been put up close by, some sort of storehouse. Basel stacked a number of metal billycans into makeshift steps and they soon reached the roof. From there it was a fairly challenging leap on to the sheer rock-face, but luckily there were plenty of foot- and handholds.

'You up to it?' he asked.

Actions spoke louder than words so she jumped, landed neatly and smiled back at him. Basel landed right beside her and scrambled swiftly up the rock. He offered her his hand to help her up on to a ledge. She accepted only so she could quickly scale the treacherous, scree-covered slope to the next ledge and offer a helping hand to him. With a rueful smile, he accepted.

'I think our bird took the next one up,' Basel said, still holding on to her fingers.

She nodded, pulled her hand away. 'Let's slow down a little. Could be dangerous.'

Cautiously they climbed up on to a shelf cut into the bare black rock. Rose could make out a hole maybe the size of a dinner plate, with little heaps of crumbled stone marking the edges. Higher up and beyond it there lay a large, messy pile of dried-out straw, sticks and husks.

'That must be its nest,' said Basel warily. 'It didn't go back there, then.'

'Needs a place with a bit more bling now,' Rose joked. 'Must have vanished off down that skylight of yours.'

'Wait.' Basel's whole body seemed to tense. 'Skylights are formed when the rock falls inwards. But there's stone chips and stuff round the outside of this one.'

Rose's eyes met his as her heart started to sink. 'So whatever made this hole was inside the cave and tunnelling out…'

Almost cheesily on cue, a blob of something like molten metal popped up from out of the hole. It kind of resembled mercury but with a golden sheen, quivering like metallic jelly. Rose and Basel took several steps backwards, almost to the edge of the ledge.

'I know it's hot here,' said Rose, 'but hot enough to melt metal?'

'It's cold in the caves,' Basel told her. 'This stuff must be what Adiel saw with…'

His voice choked off as the molten golden blob started rolling towards them, gleaming in the sunlight, leaving no marks on the rock behind it.

Time we were making tracks at any rate, she thought. But out loud she simply shouted, 'Run!'

Basel was first over the edge, but Rose was right behind him. When she reached the ledge she turned and looked up. Saw the glob somehow sticking to the rock-face as it rolled down towards them.

'What is that thing?' panted Basel.

'Dunno,' said Rose, launching herself down the next scree-scattered slope. 'But I think it's hungry.'

The rough rock tore at her clothes, stung her palms and scratched her skin as she scrambled back down, Basel right beside her. At last they reached the asphalt roof of the portakabin. Rose risked an upwards glance to find the molten metallic thing was hissing its way towards them, faster and faster.

Wild-eyed and panting for breath, Basel sprinted over to the makeshift billycan stairway. He rocketed down and Rose followed – but one of the metal canisters had been knocked loose, it gave way under her step and suddenly she was falling.

She hit the ground hard and awkwardly amid the clanging of tumbling billycans, and gasped as a shooting pain burned through her ankle.

In a moment Basel was beside her, helping her up. 'You OK? Can you walk?'

'Better hope I can run,' said Rose grimly as the molten blob appeared at the edge of the roof, pulsing with golden light.

Suddenly it flopped off the edge and landed on the baking earth. Rose backed away, ignored the biting pain in her ankle as the blob rolled towards her.

But Basel had crept behind it with one of the billycans and now he brought it down, spout first, on the golden blob, trapping it inside. 'Quick, get something we can stick on top of it!'

Rose hobbled over to grab another of the fallen canisters. She plonked it on top, then went to get more to stack around the sides. Soon the billycan was buried and still.

'Nice one, Basel,' said Rose admiringly. 'Simple but effective.'

Basel looked less sure. 'We don't know how long it'll hold that thing.'

'Let's find the Doctor. He'll be able to sort it.' She thought hard. 'But where's it come from?'

'Fynn,' said Basel with certainty. 'He's been messing round with nature too long. Something like this was bound to happen.'

'This isn't anything to do with nature,' said Rose. 'It's got to be…'

He looked at her expectantly.

'Well.' She felt suddenly embarrassed. 'It's got to be alien or something.'

He grinned. 'Yeah, right. Come on. We'll see what Fynn has to say about it.'

He set off. With a last worried glance at the pile of canisters, Rose hobbled after him.

Fynn started as the Doctor suddenly sat bolt upright. 'Are you OK?'

'Where was I?' The Doctor stared round, took a deep breath in and winced. 'Oh yes. In here, in pain and in the dark.' He looked over at the open entrance to the growth chamber. 'Could be getting lighter. When did Goldfinger step aside?'

'Not long ago,' said Fynn. 'I – I was going to go inside but…' *But I was terrified!* He looked away. 'I didn't think I should leave you here.'

'Ooh, sweet,' said the Doctor vaguely. 'What we have to ask ourselves is – why is he knocking us back one minute and welcoming us in the next? Eh? Mm? What's changed?'

'You used that tool on him. What was it?'

'Sonic screwdriver. Resonates magnetic fields, oscillates atomic structures and available in a variety of attractive colours.' The Doctor looked at Fynn. 'D'you think he responded to a bit of posh technology, is that it?'

Fynn scowled. 'You said he was dead.'

'Oh, Kanjuchi's dead, yes. The man himself, the man you employed, he's dead as a dinosaur. But his body is still in service. Question is – *whose* service?' The Doctor got up. 'And whoever or whatever's in charge, do they want to find out more about me and my posh technology, or do they want me dead? I dunno. I just dunno.' He clapped Fynn heartily on the back and grinned. 'I do a great impression of a lamb trotting off to the slaughter. Wanna see?'

'I need to find out what's happened to my crop,' said Fynn quietly.

'Let's have a look, then.' The Doctor slipped through the narrow gap between the two boulders and stepped cautiously into the growth chamber.

Fynn followed him quickly inside. 'Oh no. No!' In the red light, the crop of fungus stood gleaming as if it was made of gold. 'What's happened here?'

'This stuff has coated Kanjuchi, that vulture and now your fungus...' The Doctor shrugged. 'Maybe it's designed to target organic life.'

'Designed?'

'By a controlling intelligence.'

Fynn wiped cold sweat from his forehead. 'A controlling *alien* intelligence? Is that what you're asking me to believe?'

'I'm telling you,' the Doctor snapped. 'Down to you if you believe me or not. And fungi are classified as being closer to animal life than plant life... Perhaps this stuff isn't very discriminating.'

'But what does it *want*?'

The Doctor shrugged again. 'Maybe it's just trying to make your art look a little prettier.'

Suddenly there was a piercing shriek from above them as a bloated, enormous shape came flapping down from the rocky ceiling of the growth chamber and perched on the gleaming spires of fungus. It had a hooked, twisted beak, wings so badly distorted they had to be broken, talons like broken pitchforks. Its eyes burned, molten with malice.

'Hold very still,' the Doctor murmured. 'Looks like our vulture's come home to roost.'

'Whatever happened to Kanjuchi has happened to the bird?' Fynn whispered.

'Yes. The DNA's been reordered.' He glanced behind him. 'By that.'

Fynn peered into the crimson shadows of the growth chamber. He saw something gleaming there, slowly pulsing with white-gold light. Rocking back and forth as if in anticipation. Waiting for them.

The vulture rose into the air on its burnished, broken wings. Fynn took a few involuntary steps backwards, then caught movement behind him. The large glowing blob split into four smaller entities and started to roll forwards. Fynn recoiled and the vulture hurled itself towards him. Fynn threw his arm up over his face, then took another step back.

But the Doctor grabbed hold of him. 'It's trying to herd us into that lot,' he hissed. 'The sonic screwdriver must have made it wary. Whatever this stuff is, it's taking no chances.' The shining, cadaverous vulture flapped at him with another ear-piercing screech. 'We're trapped!'

FIVE

Fynn tore himself free of the Doctor's grip. 'You said your sonic device made this stuff wary,' he said. 'Use it again! Full power! Scare it!'

'Full power?' The Doctor stared at him in horror. 'Have you any idea how much the batteries for this thing cost?'

The vulture thrashed through the air towards them and thumped the Doctor in the chest, knocking him down. Its talons raked the air above his face. At the same time, the golden blobs surged forwards to get him.

The Doctor whipped out his little ceramic wand and held it out towards the blobs. The tip buzzed blue. The vulture descended, twisted beak wide open to tear at his fingers, but the Doctor brought up his legs and pedalled the air to keep it at bay. The blobs stopped rolling forwards, pulsed faster, quivered as if they were trembling.

'Ultrasonics,' the Doctor called cheerfully over the raucous screams of the vulture. 'Agitates the molecules. And sometimes…'

With a deafening clap, the back of the growth chamber seemed to split open like a cracked eggshell. The vulture flew backwards as if repelled by some invisible force. The various blobs of molten matter flowed back into one.

Then the warped figure of Kanjuchi appeared in the narrow opening to the chamber, struggling to squeeze his golden girth through the gap between the boulders. His fingers tore and gouged at the stone. He even started to bite it, gleaming fangs crunching through the solid rock as if it was hamburger.

'He's not scared,' Fynn shouted. 'He's livid!'

With a guttural roar and an explosion of stony shrapnel, Kanjuchi pushed through into the chamber and charged straight for the Doctor. Fynn tried to help him up, but Kanjuchi was too fast. He swatted Fynn aside – and then ran on to the back wall of the chamber. There, glinting red-gold in the dull, scarlet light, he turned and planted himself firmly in front of the gaping split in the rock, his arms raised so he completely blocked the way.

'Interesting.' The Doctor jumped up, switching off his device. 'The primary purpose of this stuff has to be defensive. It's trying to protect something – and so it's converting local animal life into sentries.' He beamed at Fynn – but then the smile faded. 'But *what's* it protecting, eh? What's so important? And what's suddenly set it off now if you opened up this chamber a while ago?' He jerked his head at the split. 'What's through there?' He took a couple of steps towards Kanjuchi and raised his voice. 'I said, what's through there?'

The golden fingers of the Kanjuchi statue curled

and clenched into enormous, lumpy fists.

'Come on, Doctor.' Skin crawling, Fynn turned quickly and headed back towards the crumbling exit. 'Before something else comes to bar our way.'

'Ignoring the problem won't make it go away, Director,' the Doctor warned him. 'Something's woken up. Something very old and very hostile. And what we're seeing are the first stirrings, that's all. It's gonna get worse, a whole lot worse. We're talking huge amounts of worse here!'

Alarmist nonsense, thought Fynn as he hurried from the chamber. He only wished he had the courage to say so out loud.

Solomon walked slowly through the darkness of the abandoned eastern caverns, his dying torch spilling a sickly yellow light over the twisting path ahead. All around were piles of rubble where ceilings had collapsed and stalagmites shattered. Some of the lava tubes were too small to walk through, you had to crouch and crawl and even wriggle on your stomach. It was small wonder the eastern tubes had been pretty much written off, at least until the fungus crop had taken hold and they needed the extra room.

Solomon reached what seemed at first sight to be a dead end in the narrow crawl-space. But the dying torch beam suggested the shadow of stones piled there, blocking the way. He flicked off the light, started to pull the rocks away.

There was a distant sound somewhere behind him and

he froze. He mustn't be found here. If he was…

The noise did not come again. Solomon returned to clearing the stones from the narrow passage ahead, then wormed his way through the gap. On this side, the passage was taller and wider.

And someone was standing at the end of the passage. A dark figure, holding a flaming torch.

'What are you doing here?' Solomon demanded.

'We want more food,' said the figure quietly.

Solomon shook his head. 'There is no more. I've told you all along, I can only give you one delivery each week.'

'It is not enough.'

'Any more would be missed.' Solomon walked towards the man with the torch and held out his hand. 'It's good to see you, Talib, but I've warned you never to come here.'

Talib accepted his hand, but his face was cold as the darkness. 'Robbers and rebels took most of the food. They took our sheep and cows, even the mats we sleep on. And they will be back.'

'I cannot give you any more,' said Solomon. 'You risk too much, coming here. If you were seen – if anyone knew the tunnels stretch as far as Gouronkah – you could find yourselves relocated to the shelters, or pushed into aid camps. Is that what you want?' He looked at Talib suspiciously. 'No. *I* know what you want. You want to find your own way through, don't you? Trying to take food for yourself.'

'We need it, Solomon.'

Solomon couldn't keep his voice from rising. 'If I'm

caught stealing for you, I'll be sent to the labour camps. And then you'll get no food, nothing – you understand? Nothing ever again.'

Angrily, Talib thrust his face up against Solomon's. 'If we do not get more we will have no need of the food. Because we will all be dead.'

'I'm sorry.' Solomon shook his head. 'I can ask Basel to speak to his friends at the Iniko camp…'

'Your father would be ashamed,' Talib sneered. 'You say you want to help your village, but –'

'I left Gouronkah fifteen years ago, yet still I'm risking everything to help you!'

'You are Fynn's now.'

Solomon didn't react. 'On Sunday,' he said slowly, 'there will be food left as usual in the marked cavern. If I think I can safely increase the amount, then I will. Now, go.'

Talib turned and stalked away, soon swallowed by the shadows.

For a good minute, Solomon stood listening to the sound of Talib's footfalls echoing away to nothing. When he was satisfied the man had gone he started to follow him, then squeezed himself into a narrow side tunnel. The floor was uneven, coated with welled-up lava. The ceiling was festooned with evil-looking stalactites left from the cooling of the molten roof. Solomon wasn't bothered by claustrophobia but in some of these passages it felt as if he was trapped inside an enormous instrument of torture.

Perhaps because he was nearing the machine.

Solomon had found it while looking for a less difficult path through the crumbling labyrinth of lava tubes; the faster he could smuggle food from out of the agri-unit, the safer for all concerned. That had been his plan.

Only now something had woken up, no one was safe. Kanjuchi was dead, and Solomon felt sick with the certainty that he would not be the last.

He turned left into another tunnel. The walls sagged here; half-melted, they mirrored his resolve. And at the end of this long, dark tunnel he could already see the magma-like glow of the machine. Why had the damn thing started glowing?

Because you found it, he told himself. *Because you woke it up*.

He turned off his torch. The excavating work in the catacombs had weakened the whole area and a crack had become a fissure. Solomon had worked on the split, enlarged it, forced a way through in the hope of finding a short cut. Instead he'd stumbled upon a secret burial chamber for… this.

Solomon stared at it: a large rectangular panel in the floor, the size of a cinema screen and made from the same gleaming, golden material as Kanjuchi and the vulture. It had been laid into the smooth surface of an ancient pool of lava and weird sculpted controls lay shimmering like molten metal on its surface. A strange, muted thrum, somewhere between the rush of a stream and the hum of a generator, sang like freshness through the fetid air. As if the panel was somehow new – not hundreds, maybe thousands, of years old.

He should have told someone, of course. Told Fynn, let it be his problem. But Fynn would want it studied, the tunnels would be crawling with experts and scientists, and he'd be lucky to get a tin of beans out to Talib once in a blue moon.

His tools still littered the tunnel. Solomon picked up his hard hat and a shock hammer and stared at the golden panel, which was glowing and humming serenely. 'Time you were hidden from sight again,' he murmured. Just a few hammer blasts and he could bring the roof down. Maybe then things would be better.

Solomon took a deep breath and released a hammering shockwave up at the ceiling of the chamber. The whole place shook around him. He risked bringing the roof down on his head as much as on the panel, but there was no alternative. Gritting his teeth, heart pounding, he fired again. This time huge clumps of the ancient rock were knocked free from the roof to shower down over the panel. But they couldn't smother its shimmering, molten light.

An awful wave of self-doubt thundered around his mind like the aftershocks of the fall-in – *it's not going to work, you've screwed up* – but he'd come too far to stop now. He bit his lip and blasted again, felt his bones jump and rattle as, with an ear-splitting crack, the roof of the chamber gave way completely. Debris rained down around him.

Solomon wasn't sure if it was his nerve that had broken or a spell the machine had cast over him. But suddenly he was running for dear life through the tunnel, playing his torch beam around the weird, warped walls of twisting passageway, praying the shockwaves wouldn't cut off his only way out.

He was running so fast, he didn't see Adiel watching him from the thickest shadows, her fingers toying with the beads about her neck.

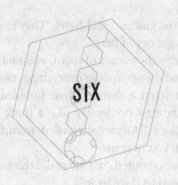

SIX

Rose followed Basel into the entrance to the growth chambers. The cave was cool and dry, and it didn't smell too good. He took a torch from a hook on the wall near the doorway and flicked on a beam of dull crimson light.

'Don't wanna disturb the bats,' he explained. 'There're thousands of them living up in the ceiling.'

'You take me to all the best places, don't you?' Even as she spoke, her foot knocked against something. 'What was that?' She recoiled, took a step back and trod on something else. 'Ugh! And that. Give me the torch!' She swiped it from him and pointed the beam down at the cavern floor. Small, golden figures lay scattered over the slimy floor.

'Oh, God,' Basel murmured. 'You know what I said about bats in the ceiling?'

She nodded. 'Looks like they've come down in the world.' Suddenly one of the little bodies started to twitch. 'Uh-oh.'

'Just like the vulture,' said Basel. 'They're coming back to life! Let's get out of here.'

'But there're thousands of them, you said. If they start flying up and dive-bombing everything, the Doctor and Fynn won't stand a chance!' Rose hobbled on into the cave, but the tiny bodies lay like a thick golden drift across the floor. 'Doctor!' she yelled, trampling over the bodies. 'Can you hear me?'

'Rose,' Basel shouted, 'whatever did this to the bats will do the same to us if we let it!'

An eerie chittering and the scissor-blade swish of wings cut through the darkness. 'Doctor, are you in there?' Rose persisted, feeling the ground start to squirm and writhe beneath her feet. A small shape went whizzing past her shoulder and she flinched. 'Doctor!'

'Yeah!' came his happy shout. 'I'm in here with Fynn. But we're coming out.'

'Hurry it up – we've got a bat situation here!' More shot past. One snagged her hair with its wings or its claws, and she swiped blindly, desperately to knock it clear.

'Look out!' Basel yelled.

There were bats everywhere, burning with fiery light. Something had sent them into a frenzy. Rose saw the Doctor dragging Fynn along by the sleeve and racing for the exit. Satisfied he was OK, she pulled her top up over her head and fled too, as fast as her throbbing ankle would allow. The air was thick with bats, snagging on her clothes, smacking into her arms and legs. *They're just mice with wings*, she told herself. *Weird, mutant golden mice with wings, yeah, but…*

She felt dizzy, disorientated, and was desperately clinging on to consciousness for fear of falling headlong into the mess of writhing bodies on the ground. Then suddenly she felt arms about her, guiding her along. 'Doctor?'

The next minute Rose felt the heat of the sun on her bare arms, baking her gooseflesh in moments. She saw Fynn dabbing at a cut to his cheek, Basel lying flat on his back on the ground, chest heaving – and found the Doctor grinning into her face.'What were you doing, coming in after me?'

'Don't say anything about me being batty,' she warned him. He looked wounded. Then he started to open his shirt and she saw he *was* wounded. 'How'd you get that bruise?' she asked him.

'More interestingly, how did I get *this* little feller?' He pulled out a small, golden creature from inside his shirt, cupped in one hand. 'Funny you should ask! Well, when I was younger I was a demon batsman. Handy in later life when you meet demon bats.' He pulled out his glasses, flicked them open and pushed them into place. 'Think I'll call him Tolstoy. Looks like a Tolstoy, don't you reckon? Hello, Tolstoy! Who's a pretty little golden boy, then?' He grinned at her. 'Easier to study than the vulture – and packs less of a punch than Kanjuchi.'

Basel looked over at them. 'The vulture got away.'

'We know,' said Fynn shakily.

'And this lump of gold stuff,' Rose continued, 'must be the stuff Adiel was talking about – it attacked us.'

'It wanted to convert you,' the Doctor said.

'We trapped it inside a billycan,' said Basel.

'If it *stayed* trapped, it had a good reason.' The Doctor looked down at his bat. 'Better get this little fella somewhere secure. Fynn, now's your chance to play the good boss. Send the staff away for their own protection. Send them home. Nice early night and a cup of Horlicks, oooh, lovely.' There was a steely edge to his tone. 'This place has to be shut down.'

'I'm not going home!' Basel protested.

'And I can't shut this unit down,' said Fynn. 'The work is too important.' He sighed. 'But I suppose non-essential personnel can be dismissed for the day…'

Rose looked at him. 'Think this will all be sorted by tomorrow morning, then, do you?'

'Not by standing round here talking about it,' Fynn said drily. 'Doctor, that creature –'

'Tolstoy.'

'– must be analysed quickly, before it can mutate and enlarge. We must take it to the laboratory. Adiel can help prepare…' He frowned. 'Is Adiel all right?'

Basel was getting to his feet. 'Left her in the common room. She was sleeping.'

'Not any more,' Rose observed.

Adiel was hurrying down the bark-chip path towards them, dreadlocks bouncing about her shoulders, face clouded with confusion.

'What's been happening?' she asked.

'You're supposed to be sedated,' Basel told her. 'I gave you a p-pill!'

'Yeah, in a fruit shot that's half-caffeine, half-taurine,'

Adiel shot back, 'like that's going to work. I wake up and suddenly everyone's gone, the common-room window's shattered, nobody's about...' She looked at Fynn. 'Kanjuchi – is he all right?'

'No.' The Doctor smiled sympathetically, but shook his head. 'I could be kind and say Kanjuchi's not himself. But I don't want to patronise you, don't want to give you false hope – and I don't want anyone to think there's the slightest chance of survival if one of those golden blobs touches you.'

'So he's really dead, then,' said Basel quietly. 'Dead and gone.'

'Not gone,' said the Doctor. 'Something else is controlling his body now. Something with a very particular purpose that's woken up under that volcano, thinking it needs to recruit sentries. We need to know more about it and fast – before anyone or anything else leaves this world with a golden handshake.' He marched up to Fynn and shook the bat in his face. 'Shall we get on?'

Rose sat in the laboratory, waiting for the Doctor to dazzle his dwindling audience with the results of his poking about. He was using the sonic screwdriver on the data-get, trying to get more out of it, she supposed. Frantic thumping and scratching were coming from a lead-lined box as the bat did its best to escape from captivity.

Fynn was hunched up over a funny-looking microscope, checking stuff out, while Adiel got busy mixing and fixing solutions in beakers. All Rose could do was clock the way Adiel acted around Fynn; her whole body seemed to go rigid any time he came near her. Maybe something had happened between them – unhappy romance, or maybe he'd passed her over for promotion, or...

Rose sighed. What did it matter? She hated feeling so useless, but suspected that even had she passed Chemistry GCSE she would still be just a mile or two out of her depth. She wished now she had gone with Basel and Solomon, rounding up the workers and sending them home early before finishing checking the unit for dodgy mutant wildlife. But she had an ankle slathered in twenty-second-century miracle cream and it was already feeling a lot better for being rested on a lab stool.

'So this golden stuff,' she began.

'Magma form,' the Doctor corrected her.

'All right, this magma form. Will it come after us? Are we gonna be invaded by golden blobs?'

The Doctor buzzed a bit more with the screwdriver. 'Know what I think? I think that it thinks that we are the invaders.'

'Can you reverse the effect – turn the bat back to normal?'

'Dunno.' He put down the data-get. 'These magma forms must secrete some substance that alters the host DNA entirely, converting the skin into a kind of flexible metal. And when the secondary mutation kicks in...'

Taking that as a cue, Adiel called up the output from an X-ray scanner pointing at the lead box.

Rose shuddered at the image on the plasma screen. Little Tolstoy had mutated like the vulture into a hideous, bloated caricature of its former self. Its wings were burnished gold, one almost twice the size of the other. Its teeth and claws had lengthened. Its eyes were wide and aglow like white-hot metal.

'Golem,' announced the Doctor suddenly, whipping off his glasses.

'What?' Rose frowned. 'The creepy thing from *Lord of the Rings*?'

'No, *golem*. A living being created from clay.' He was staring at the shifting, blue-black shadows on the X-ray screen. 'A crude, primitive servant. Not crude as in it goes round shouting "Knickers!" all the time; crude as in roughly made, unfinished. Once brought to life by mystical incantations, it acts unthinkingly, unswervingly, for its master.'

Adiel watched him, her dark eyes wide. 'You think that's what Kanjuchi and the transformed animals have become?'

He nodded. 'Only remade from magma, not mud.'

'And using alien technology instead of magic spells?' Rose ventured.

Fynn stared at them both in despair. 'You make it sound as if you deal with things like this every day!'

Rose and the Doctor nodded in perfect unison. 'Yeah.'

'Question is,' the Doctor added, 'how long has this stuff been cooking up? The tektites on Adiel's necklace – legacy of that meteor… We're talking old, really old. Really, really, really, really, reallllllllllly old.'

Rose lowered her voice. 'But what about that space pollution the TARDIS picked up around here? That's recent, isn't it?'

'*Really* recent. Really, really, realllllllllly –'

'Which means there's been a spaceship in the area!'

The Doctor grinned. 'Which could explain why this stuff has started reacting! It doesn't like technology; it *hated* it when I started sonicking…'

'What are you two talking about now?' Fynn demanded.

'We need to know why this stuff has decided to start shaping the local animal life into golems, right?' said the Doctor, rubbing his hands together. 'So we need to know what's in those uncharted caves.'

'You can't go back in there,' Adiel blurted.

Fynn was quick to agree. 'We barely got out alive the last time.'

"S'all right, keep your pants on!' The Doctor gave them both a cocky smile and waggled the data-get. 'I've fiddled with the scan-sensors on this, increased the range and sensitivity to full capacity. If we can insert some memory wafers, hook it up to an output screen, we should be able to build up a clearer picture of what's sitting underneath that volcano.'

'Those devices are extremely expensive, Doctor,' said Fynn, snatching the data-get and training it on Adiel. 'If your tampering has…' He trailed off as a keen whine of power bit into the atmosphere. He studied the meter. 'Incredible. Even at minimum scan, the volume of data –'

'– will swamp its built-in memory, which is why we

need the wafers.' The Doctor leaned in over his shoulder and stabbed a couple of buttons, powering it down. 'Well, well – according to this… Adiel's a little bit alien.'

'What?' Adiel stared at him, shifting on the spot uncomfortably. 'What are you talking about?'

'I'd say it's those tektites round your neck,' the Doctor went on. 'Yep, the composition's definitely alien, sure as eggs is eggs. Those stones weren't formed in a meteor impact. They came from the forced landing of an alien spaceship.'

Fynn disentangled himself, his face disapproving. 'Doctor, really…'

'Really, really, really, realllllllly…' His deep brown eyes were agleam as he walked up to Adiel. 'You say you got those pretty stones from round here?'

She nodded. 'The women at Gouronkah find them and sell them.'

'Gouronkah?' Rose wondered. It sounded more alien than some of the places the Doctor took her.

'A backwards little settlement nearby,' Fynn explained. 'The locals tend to be… intolerant of staff from the agri-units. See us as violating the land, the old traditions.' He frowned. 'Why would you wish to consort with such people, Adiel?'

Adiel shrugged, and Rose caught the coldness in her dark eyes. 'I believe my vacation time is my own, Director.'

'May I see the stones?' the Doctor asked, holding out his hand.

A little reluctantly, she passed him the necklace. And

as she did so, the lead box suddenly jumped with a violent scrape across the table-top, making everyone skitter.

'Whatever's underneath the volcano, that thing in there's pretty keen to get back,' said Rose shakily.

'Director Fynn, I need to take a rest period,' Adiel said abruptly.

Fynn nodded, distracted again by his souped-up data-get. 'Thirty minutes, no more. We need to start imaging that volcano.' He looked at the Doctor. 'This will be of untold value to the project. We can accurately survey the entire lava-tube network from the outside, increase user access and harvesting efficiency…'

'Yeah, hello, Director?' The Doctor made a pair of scissors with his fingers. 'Cut.'

Not meeting anyone's gaze, Adiel swept across the room to the far door.

The Doctor went over to Rose, put on a smile. 'Give her a few minutes,' he said under his breath so Fynn wouldn't hear, 'then go after her.'

'Worried I might be getting lonely?' said Rose.

The Doctor shook his head. 'Worried *she* might be getting up to something.'

In the pink-red glare of the setting sun, Solomon stood at the edge of the east fields and watched the guards talking at the main gate. The day shift would soon be drifting back to their homes in Condo City Three, or to the dive clubs, casinos and bars they preferred to kill time in.

In many ways, the new cities were every bit as dirty

and dangerous as the camps and shanties they had been thrown up to replace. Solomon thought of the comfortless cement block he'd been assigned when he'd first started working for the agri-units. The toilets backed up and the tap water was undrinkable. The whole district smelt of sewage and all residents were on a waiting list to move to better accommodation on the east edge.

Three years later Solomon was still waiting.

'Hey, Solomon, man,' said Nadif, shuffling amiably along, raising small clouds of sand in his wake. 'You off duty too?'

'Nah,' he said mildly, still watching the chatting guards, carefree in their ignorance. 'Looks like I'm here to stay.'

'Bad luck, my friend. Reckon we could all use a drink after what we've seen today.' He paused, troubled. 'Fynn and his type will explain it all away, right?'

'Uh-huh. You wait.'

Apparently reassured, Nadif nodded and set off for the main gate. 'Be seeing you.'

Solomon nodded. 'Guess you will.'

Where else would he be? His father had said he could come home – to the family home – any time he wanted. But Dad had died the same way he had lived, in hardship and poverty, because he stayed true to the old traditions, the old ways. Solomon didn't want that for his sons. He wanted them to have a shot at the chances in life that his ID pass had ruled out for him from birth. If you were born in an old-style village – or Native Settlement (Primitive) in the new-speak – then you had to fight tooth and nail and wait for ever for even the most basic urban upgrades. Solomon had taken thirteen years to work his way up from labour grade nobody to Chief Overseer, selling himself to the likes of Fynn for peanuts – but it was worth every cent he never saw. Now his sons were graded urban sector, attended speed schools, would have their own bank accounts some day – would stand a chance of getting out of the poverty trap and into a better life for themselves somewhere else.

So long as their daddy wasn't exposed as a thief. So long as he didn't wind up in a labour camp because he couldn't turn his back on his old birthplace and his father's ghost.

So long as the golden death didn't come for them all.

Solomon spat on the floor and watched the sun slowly sinking behind Mount Tarsus. 'Please, God,' he murmured as the sky went on darkening, 'don't let others suffer for my sins.'

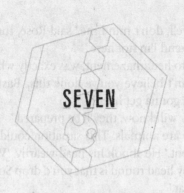

SEVEN

Rose made her way to the common room. The broken windows had been boarded up with planks of wood. Only a little clear glass remained to hint at the beautiful African nightscape.

Adiel and Basel were leaning forward on separate couches, talking in low voices. When Rose walked in they looked up guiltily, like they were whispering dirty secrets.

'Just fancied a fruit shot,' said Rose vaguely, crossing to the fridge. 'Everyone sent home who needs to be?'

Basel nodded. "Cept me.'

'Everything OK?'

'Sure,' said Basel, in a tone that suggested it wasn't.

She pointed to her bad foot. 'Mind if I drink the fruit shot here? Need to rest the ankle.'

Adiel looked meaningfully at Basel and shrugged. 'We can speak Kenga,' she said.

'That's nice for you,' said Rose blankly.

Basel's expression was apologetic. 'Conversation's sort of personal.'

'Yeah, well, don't mind me,' said Rose, turning to her drink. 'Pretend I'm not here.'

Which, to her amazement, was exactly what they did.

'I just can't believe you've done this,' Basel muttered. 'People are gonna get hurt.'

'Security will know, they'll be prepared.'

'That lot are animals! This situation could go belly up in a moment.' He shook his head wearily. 'What I really can't get my head round is that you'd drop Solomon in it, just like that.'

'I have to,' Adiel said simply. 'It's for the greater good.'

'Act like an activist, talk like a scientist,' he sneered.

'I don't see why you're not happier. You told me yourself that you were after something that could get you publicity.'

'Yeah, the right kind of publicity – like catching a solid-gold vulture,' Basel agreed, loud as you like. 'Something that'll draw attention to what places like this are doing to the environment. Something small enough to smuggle out of the unit before Fynn starts covering everything up.'

Rose stared at them, gobsmacked. So that was why Basel had been so keen to catch the golden vulture – and quite happy to let her risk her life helping him. What she couldn't believe was the way they were chatting about all this like she didn't exist, like she wasn't even worth their secrecy.

'Exactly,' said Adiel. 'If this alien golem stuff is really true, the government will put this whole place under wraps, top secret, all of that.' She looked at Basel. 'But a story like this, this is *news*. If I'm going to get Fynn investigated –'

'Listen to yourself!' Basel shook his head like he was disgusted. 'Don't pretend you're doing this for Gouronkah. This is about you.'

Rose couldn't stay quiet any longer. 'What are you two on about?'

'Told you, Rose, it's personal.' Basel turned back to Adiel. 'Whatever happens, State Guards will end up searching the tunnels, find out what Solomon's been up to – and pack him off to a labour camp.'

'If he's got secret links to this glowing stuff, then maybe he deserves it!'

'*What?*' Rose said, more loudly.

'He'd never do something like that!' Basel insisted. 'He's straight. You know damn well that without him everyone in Gouronkah would have starved to death. He's risked his whole life for them –'

'They don't need handouts,' Adiel insisted, more animated now than Rose had ever seen her. 'They need their independence.'

'Independence won't fill your belly,' said Basel wearily, 'whatever your student mates might say. And if you think I'm gonna stand by while you sell Solomon down the river –'

'I hadn't realised you were so close.' Adiel's voice was growing colder. 'Well, I'm telling you, he went straight to this golden panel – he knew it was there.'

'You *what?*' said Rose, whose chin was almost scraping the floor by now.

Adiel ignored the outburst. 'And then he tried to bring the roof down on it!'

'How come you were even there, spying on him, anyway?' Basel challenged. 'When we left you, you were sleeping.'

'My watch alarm went off – I had to keep my meeting. I came to, saw those windows all broken.' She looked genuinely troubled. 'I got worried, wandered out… Then I saw Solomon going into the tunnels and I followed him.'

'What meeting's this? What've you been up to?' Rose demanded.

Finally, they both took notice.

Adiel peered at Rose like she was something under one of Fynn's slides. 'You understood what we said?'

'Not exactly hard to get the gist, is it?' Rose folded her arms. 'Can't see Fynn making either of you employee of the month when he finds out.'

'She speaks Kenga,' said Basel disbelievingly.

'A teenage white girl is fluent in an African dialect barely spoken outside of northern Chad?' Adiel's gaze hardened further. 'Just who *are* you?'

'Erm…' Rose realised the TARDIS translators had just stitched her up good and proper. 'I'm, um, good at languages.'

'She's got to be press,' said Adiel, then corrected herself, looked meaningfully at Basel. 'No, not press. She's a bio-pirate, sent here by another agri-unit, one of Fynn's rivals.' She put on a sarcastic tone of voice. 'Come to see what she can steal away from Africa for the good

74

of Western society.'

Her words had the desired effect on Basel and his face twisted into a sneer. 'Is that true?' He took a menacing step towards her. 'Rose?'

'Come off it!' Rose wasn't about to be intimidated; she took a step towards *him*. 'If I was any sort of journalist or pirate or whatever, would I have given myself away as dumbly as that? Don't think so.'

'So who are you really, you and this Doctor? How come you know so much about all this weird stuff?'

'Sounds as if we don't, not yet.' She took another two steps towards him. 'So how about you tell me everything that's been going on? Maybe the Doctor can help.'

'This isn't your business,' said Adiel coldly.

'Sounds like it's everyone's business.' Rose gave her a challenging glare. 'So should I go tell Fynn the stuff I *do* know? Or do you want to take us straight to this golden panel?'

'Those tunnels aren't safe for anyone,' said Adiel. 'Not now.'

Rose looked at each of them in turn and then made to leave. 'The Doctor needs to know about this.'

'Wait,' said Adiel, catching hold of Rose's arm. 'I'm sorry. You're right. The golden thing could be important. But what if I *did* imagine it? I mean, I was suffering from shock and dosed up on p-pills when I saw it. We don't want to delay the Doctor's imaging the chambers in the volcano to come with us on a wild-goose chase.'

Basel raised his eyebrows. 'Changing your tune, aren't you?'

Or calling *the tune*, Rose thought to herself as Adiel attempted an innocent shrug. 'So what're you saying?'

'Maybe we should check it out by ourselves,' said Adiel.

Not that anything sus is going on round here, of course, thought Rose. But the idea of taking a quick shufti and finding out more did appeal. She could actually make herself useful while the Doctor took care of the science bit.

Rose put her weight on her bad ankle – it hurt, but it held – and gestured to the door. 'What're we waiting for?' she said. 'Let's go.'

Fynn finished expanding the data-get's memory wafers just as the Doctor re-entered the lab, his sharp features tugged down in a frown. 'Funny. Well, not so much funny as peculiar. Funny peculiar.'

'What is?'

'No sign of Rose or Adiel.'

'I told Adiel no more than thirty minutes.' Fynn considered. 'It's not like her to disobey a directive.'

'She's been through a lot lately,' the Doctor reflected, picking up the girl's necklace from the workbench.

'Did you analyse that properly?'

'Yes,' he said simply. 'Traces of the creeping magma in some of the tektites, so it definitely came from the same place as our golem-maker. But hopefully there's not enough in there to be a threat.'

'Adiel's been wearing it long enough,' said Fynn.

'So she has.' The Doctor shoved the necklace into his

trouser pocket. 'You all set with the data-get?'

Fynn nodded and passed it over. 'I've snapped in five googol wafers and set it to remote output so we can monitor the results on the viewer.' Then he cleared his throat. 'I… I am not used to asking for help, Doctor, or to giving thanks when it's offered.'

The Doctor beamed at him. 'That's all right, big fella. It's the planet I'm doing this for, not you and your mushrooms…' He tailed off, as if distracted. 'Was that rude? Sorry if that was a bit rude.'

'We are both working for the sake of the planet, Doctor,' Fynn said quietly. 'I have to see my dream through. So please, tell me truthfully – are you confident you can put right whatever's gone wrong here?'

'Modesty forbids that I answer that question – oh, all right then, yes. Yes! Yes, of course I can!' He checked over his new imager. 'Given time. Time and space to work, and assuming no one else starts pushing their nose in. Oh, and that I'm not killed before I've finished.' He looked at Fynn. 'Don't suppose you've launched any spaceships or orbital probes round here lately, have you?'

'Spaceships?' Fynn frowned. 'Of course not.'

'Afraid you'd say that. Means we've got visitors. Visitors who've parked outside and are waiting in the car.' He started pacing round in a small circle. 'And judging by the ion fumes up in the atmosphere, they've left the engines running. Why are they waiting? Waiting for someone to come out? Or for someone to return…' He threw his head back and laughed suddenly, then shook his head. 'This is hopeless. Rubbish! Got to find out more. Director Fynn, do you have a flash car?'

'I have my own transport. Why?'

'I can see you're a driven man and I could do with some driving myself.' He grinned. 'Once around the volcano, that's what we need.'

Fynn bristled. 'I am not being your chauffeur, Doctor.'

'Then be my secretary,' the Doctor suggested. 'Call up Solomon so he can take me instead. Only do it fast, yeah? I don't know how much time we have left.'

'Before what?'

'Before our visitors turn off the engines and come knocking on Mount Tarsus's door,' said the Doctor, striding from the room. 'Whatever they've come for, it has to be inside that volcano. But have they come because it's woken up – or has it woken up because they've come?'

The billycan Basel had placed over the magma blob finally shook so much that it disturbed the canisters stacked on top of it. They tumbled to the ground in a clattering heap.

The magma form had long since tunnelled away. But the creatures it had transformed below ground had lingered, tiny lives frozen while alien proteins reworked their cells. Now they were ready to move again.

Hundreds of gleaming bodies swarmed up from the earth, their twisted legs clanging against the warm metal, huge, bent pincers opening and closing like scissors, puncturing the surface of the cans. Soon, thousands more were pouring out from behind the storehouse.

They went on gathering in greater and greater numbers.

In life the driver ants had fought unthinkingly for queen and colony. But now they were working for a higher power.

The night was only a little cooler than the day, and just as dusty. The sky was a rich purple-black, like a new bruise, swelling over the crops, the volcano and the distant dunes and mountains.

Rose did her best to keep up with the others, rubbing grit from her eyes and determined not to let on how much her ankle hurt. The moon was broad and big above, comfortingly familiar in a strange place and time, its silvery light drowned by the lantern-posts set along the paths of the compound. Basel kept looking round nervously, as if he expected something nasty to come hurtling out of the crop field. But Adiel kept staring straight ahead, walking quickly.

They reached a large metal door set into a rocky slope. Adiel keyed in a code and it opened on to darkness. She flicked a switch and red light seeped out from circular lamps in the tunnel walls.

'Can we leave the door unlocked?' Rose asked a little nervously.

'Yes,' said Adiel, passing them each a torch. 'That's a good idea. Come on. It's this way.'

Rose and Basel followed her, traipsing along through the cool, crimson gloom. The passage widened and the slippery mess beneath Rose's feet told her she was back in bat territory. Then the lights stopped, and they all flicked on their torches. The blood-red shadows grew thicker, shifting all around them. Rose's eyes kept trying to make sense of the weird, twisted rock formations, finding monstrous faces and staring, misshapen eyes. It was horrible. But Adiel was not distracted. She didn't waver once on her convoluted course.

'Knows her way around, doesn't she?' Rose whispered.

'Yeah. How many times you been down here, Adiel?' Basel demanded. 'There's been no development work in this area for almost a year.'

'That's what we're supposed to believe,' said Adiel mysteriously. She stopped by a side tunnel. 'It's through here – the golden panel I told you about. Go check it.'

Wielding his torch like a weapon, Basel ducked under a set of toothy stalactites and crept along the narrow passage. Rose kept close behind him.

Solomon swung the pick-up round the bumpy dirt track that skirted the volcano, trying to miss the largest potholes. The Doctor was balancing in the back, pointing his gadget at the steep slopes like it was an old film camera, laughing and shouting, *'Bellissimo!'* every few seconds. 'Work with me, baby! Yes, come on, you know you want to!'

'Are you seeing inside?' Solomon called to him.

'Imaging very nicely, ta,' the Doctor informed him.

'What's there?'

'Not sure. So much data – tons of the stuff! But mushrooms apart, I don't think it's organic.'

'Huh?'

'Not living. Not alive.'

Solomon felt a little happier. 'So it's dead, then?'

Suddenly the sky lit up as if lightning was striking – striking again and again in quick succession. The world became bleached out bright and white. Dazzled, Solomon stamped on the brakes. The Doctor was thrown forwards on to his face. The engine coughed and died, and the light bled quickly from the night.

'What was that?' Solomon whispered, staring round, afraid.

The night sky was silent and clear, no storm impending, no planes or choppers up there.

The Doctor picked himself up from the dusty floor of the pick-up. 'I don't know,' he said, peering at his little screen. 'But it gave the volcano a fright.'

Solomon turned to him angrily. 'Could you be serious just for once?'

'The data-get picked up a massive energy surge,' he said over the noisy ticking of the engine as it started to cool. 'Not only from that lightning-flash effect but from inside Mount Tarsus.'

Rose followed Basel through the tunnel, focusing on his crimson butt bobbing in front of her. It wasn't a brilliant view, but the best available. The walls seemed to be closing in on them, distorted faces leering out from the dark rock.

Suddenly Basel stopped.

'What is it?' said Rose breathlessly, craning to see past him.

'Dead end,' he reported. 'There's nothing!'

Rose spun round, started to make her way back. 'Adiel, you've got the wrong –'

Bang. She bumped into something that wasn't there, and Basel bumped into the back of her.

A dark silhouette appeared in the muddy, bloody light.

'Adiel, what the hell is this?' Basel stormed, striking his fist against the invisible barrier.

'Roof prop,' she informed him. 'A simple cushion of charged air between ground and –'

'I know, it's a construction tool,' he snapped. 'Now turn it off so we can get out.'

'I can't let you go yet, it's too important,' she said, the weird acoustics taking her whisper and making it something low, cold, almost inhuman. 'Rose, you'd tell the Doctor, who would tell Fynn –'

'He's not like that!' Rose started.

'– and Basel, you might try to interfere to keep Solomon out of the firing line.'

'When that lot get here we're all in the firing line!' he protested.

'I can't take any chances.'

'You're taking one hell of a chance,' Basel hissed back, 'and everyone's lives are at risk. You'll need the State Guards to take care of that lot.'

'What lot?' Rose banged uselessly on the wall of air herself. 'Will someone just tell me what's going on?'

'The attack will come in the next few hours,' Adiel continued. 'You're well clear of the route they'll take to reach the compound. In any case, they won't be able to get through the barrier. It's set to switch off in eight hours' time or at my override, whichever comes first.'

'We might not have enough air for eight hours!' Basel argued.

'C'mon, Adiel,' said Rose, trying to stay calm. 'This is stupid, yeah? We'll keep quiet if that's what you –'

'Yes,' she said. 'I think you should keep quiet and not draw attention to yourselves.' Then she turned and walked quickly away. 'I'm sorry,' she called back over her shoulder. 'This will all be finished soon.'

'Come back!' Basel kicked the invisible shield. 'Let us out!'

'Pack it in,' Rose told him. 'You'll use up our air faster.'

'She can't do this to us!' He kicked the rock wall instead – then jumped about, holding his foot and swearing.

'I'm swooning at your manliness,' said Rose drily. 'Just calm down and tell me – what is she on about? *What* attack? What's going –'

He rounded on her, trembling with anger – or maybe fear. 'Local villagers, right? Starving to death, and what little they've got is taken off them by bandits, robbers, murderers – organised into rebel groups against central government. And the village is built right over some of these tunnels.'

'And what, Solomon's been using them to get food out to the villagers?' she asked. 'Trying to help?'

'Right. But the wrong kind of help as far as Adiel and her well-educated mates are concerned. They want to get the rebels locked up, out the picture. Standing up to the government is fine, but not when you're killing innocent people to do it.'

Rose remembered the accusations levelled at her and the Doctor when they arrived. 'So *she's* an activist!'

'This is about more than just politics. She's always had it in for Fynn. It's like she blames him for something.' He sighed and shook his head. 'I dunno. She won't let anyone close…'

'Sounds like whoever's attacking's gonna be *too* close to us,' Rose prompted him. 'What have we got to look forward to?'

'Adiel told the village leader – Talib, his name is – to make sure those robbers and bandits saw him coming down here, knowing they'd follow him. Knowing they'd find out about this place.' He shook his head. 'They're starving too – so why settle for stealing Solomon's free handouts when they can get into the unit through these tunnels and take all the food they want by force?'

Rose understood. 'Only she'll have tipped off security, who'll be ready for them.'

'I've heard Solomon talking about those rebels. Some of them, after all that time on the run… they're animals, Rose. Killers.' He slammed his palm against the invisible barrier once again. 'They ain't about to come quietly.'

'And that's happening tonight?'

'According to Talib's spies. Adiel came here to meet him like she'd arranged – and that's when she saw Solomon.'

'Playing with his golden panel.' Rose bit her lip. 'At least, that's her story.'

Basel frowned. 'What d'you mean?'

'She was acting sort of strange, wasn't she? And that necklace…' She forced an airy shrug and a smile. 'Oh, well. Bandits and murderers, that's not so bad, is it? It's almost a relief. Thought she was possessed, but now we know she's just bonkers.'

'What are you on about?'

Rose shrugged. 'Well, I was starting to think she came down here to meet…'

Her voice dried in her throat as a bizarre, misshapen silhouette stole into sight around the corner of the narrow passage.

'…aliens,' Rose concluded, wishing she'd kept her big gob shut.

The creature's head was thin and spiked like a cactus. Its neck was fat like a giant toad's, billowing out and then sucking back in. Two spindly arms stuck out on either side of the blobby body, each ending in a heavy-duty pincer like a crab's. Its many legs were thin and clacked together like a bundle of dry sticks.

Rose was glad she couldn't make out the finer details of the alien's anatomy as it scuttled across the blood-red stone towards them.

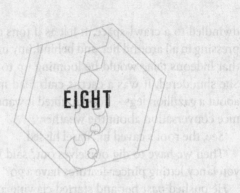

EIGHT

Rose recoiled from the creature, but Basel just stood there, staring in shock.

'What the hell is that thing?' he croaked.

'Dunno. But it's all right, we're safe,' she told him, forcing a smile. 'There's Adiel's invisible wall thing, remember? We can't get out, but that thing can't get in.'

The silent, shadowy creature produced a tubular object from somewhere, clamped carefully in one of its pincers. It pointed the tube at the roof prop generator and a green glow appeared. A worrying fizzing noise started up from ground level.

'Great,' said Rose. '*Lock-picking* crab-cactus thing.' She turned and started running back down the tunnel. 'Come on.'

Basel stared after her. 'But it's a dead end,' he protested.

'It's dead *us* if we don't find a way through. Come *on!*'

The shadows blurred and shifted in the red glare of the torch as they pelted down the narrow passage. Soon Rose was on her knees, shuffling along as the tunnel dwindled to a crawl-space. It felt as if tons of rock were pressing in all around her, and behind, any moment now, that hideous *thing* would be looming up to do... what? She shuddered. It was a cactus-crab toad monster with about a gazillion legs – Rose doubted it wanted to start a nice conversation about the weather.

'See, the roof's caved in,' Basel hissed.

'Then we have to dig ourselves out,' said Rose. 'Or do you fancy letting pincer-features have a go?'

He pushed past her and started clawing at the packed pile of rubble, faster and faster.

'Yes!' Rose hissed as he pulled away a large chunk of rock, reaching in to help clear the pile of smaller stones it had dislodged. But suddenly she realised something had changed. It wasn't that she could hear something – her ears were adjusting to the *absence* of sound. 'Oh, God. That thing's turned off the barrier. It'll be coming.'

Clack-clacketty-clack...

Rose felt her nails breaking, her fingers bleeding as she scratched at the rock pile, or at Basel's hands when they got in the way. They worked in terrified silence, little whimpers building at the back of Basel's throat. Another slab of stone came free.

'That's enough for us to wriggle through,' Rose declared. 'Get going.'

'You go first,' said Basel. 'Then if I get stuck, you can pull me through.'

There was no time to argue. Rose dived into the narrow hole they had made, felt the rock dig into her shoulders and scuff the bare flesh at the top of her arms.

But the thought of that bristling shadow falling over her pushed her on. She gritted her teeth, sucked in her stomach and hauled herself through, heart banging like a bass bin in a club. To her relief, there was actually somewhere to go; the tunnel seemed to open up a bit.

'Quick,' Rose shouted, scouting ahead a little way. The tunnel curled round to the right. 'Come *on*, Basel!' She turned to find his head pushed through the gap, and a few moments later his shoulders had cleared too. But then he stopped, gasped with pain. 'Has it got you?'

'My wallet's digging in,' he croaked.

'Never mind that!'

'You don't know *where* it's digging in!'

She grabbed hold of his arms and heaved with all her strength. 'I'll do a lot worse to you if you don't get – on – with – *it*!'

He burst out through the crevice like a banana squeezed from its skin – shrieking as he did so.

Rose crouched down beside him. 'You OK? Did I hurt you?'

Basel got up painfully. Rose saw that his bare leg was cut and bleeding. 'That thing got hold of me,' he said shakily. 'Almost took my ankle off. What the hell is –'

There was a loud, cracking noise from the crawl-space. Suddenly a pincer pushed through, slicing and snapping at the air.

Basel yelped, and Rose grabbed hold of his hand and dragged him down the passageway behind her.

Into hell.

Rose skidded to a stop, stared around in horror,

clutched his hand tighter for comfort. The passage had widened into a cave dark as night and strewn with skeletons. Thick, fluffy mould hugged the bare bones like cobwebs. Everywhere her blood-red torchlight fell, sightless sockets stared back at her.

'What is this?' she whispered, a sick feeling rising up from her stomach.

'Must be that thing's trophy room,' Basel hissed.

From the tunnel behind them, the horrible clacking of the creature's feet on the bare rock grew louder and faster.

Fynn was attempting to write a journal of the day's bizarre events, pausing every couple of words just to stare numbly at the things he was writing, when the lead box containing the bat almost leaped off the workbench. Like it was trying to break out of its cell and be free...

Gingerly, he pushed the heavy container back into the centre of the bench. Then he turned and left the lab, spooked. He went to lab block reception and grabbed a two-way radio, suddenly anxious there was good back-up out there should they need it. 'Main gate, this is Director Fynn, do you copy?'

Static crowded out of the radio, no voices, no signal at all.

'Main gate, repeat, this is Director Fynn...'

He heard the distant sound of breaking glass. The static sounded even louder. Cursing under his breath, Fynn changed the frequency. 'Solomon, are you receiving me?'

Nothing.

Cursing again, Fynn went out into the hot, starlit night. Sand blew about, stinging his exposed skin, coating his lips. He hurried towards the main gate. If he found that the guards' radios were turned off or faulty he would put a rocket the size of a Saturn V up their…

Fynn staggered to a halt. A sick feeling thrilled through him.

The guards' radios might well be working. But the guards themselves had been frozen into life-sized, gleaming gold statues, clothes and all. Six of them huddled together beside the sentry hut in various stages of panic. Fynn stumbled backwards in fear as the men suddenly lurched apart, taking up positions in front of the main gate like they meant business. Clearly no one else was coming in, and no one was getting out.

'Doctor! Solomon!' Fynn was almost dribbling into the two-way radio. 'Are you receiving me?'

Static still, like the sound of stars being scratched out of the sky.

Then he caught sluggish movement. A golden blob, undulating towards him from behind the sentry hut.

Heart pounding, Fynn found himself changing course and haring headlong into the wide-open night, towards the volcano.

'Keep looking for another way out,' Rose urged Basel. If only the damned torches were brighter. Telling a shadow from a crevice was next to impossible and Rose wound up feeling along the walls, stumbling over the skeletons, desperation rising.

'There *was* a way out here, look,' Basel called miserably. 'But it's caved in. Completely sealed.'

'Good. That route leads away from the volcano,' came a weird, high, rattling voice that seemed to crunch up the words like crisps. 'I want to go deeper inside.'

The alien had caught up with them.

Rose risked shining her torch on it. The thing didn't flinch, but she and Basel did.

What she'd taken for cactus spines were actually eyelashes, long and bristly, which formed circles around five piggy little eyes. They were arranged like spots on a dice in the middle of the alien's bud-shaped head. It had a bulbous nose and a small slash for a mouth. Incongruously, it seemed to be wearing a dark suit. A bow tie was fastened loosely round its puffed-up neck, and its shirt and jacket had four enormously flared sleeves – whether as a fashion statement or simply to allow its pincers through, Rose had no idea. In contrast, the 'trousers' it wore were skin-tight; the morass of legs reminded her of bristles on a brush, bending and flexing and clacking together as the creature shifted its weight about.

'What are you?' she whispered, beckoning Basel over towards her.

'*Who* am I, thank you very much,' the creature corrected her. 'I am an individual, you know. Extremely individual.' It clattered about in a circle. 'Few are more individual than I!'

'You certainly stand out a bit,' Rose agreed.

'My name is Jaxamillian Faltato,' it said primly,

dropping a small bead on the floor that glowed a bright, sulphurous yellow, lighting the cavern. 'You are natives, I take it.'

'That thing can speak Arabic too,' whispered Basel, standing beside her now, eyes wide with shock. 'It's from space. How'd it learn to do that?'

'It? It is a *he*!' Faltato shimmied with annoyance. 'How dare you challenge my masculinity! As for your silly language, that is child's play. One needs only a single tongue and two lips to speak it.'

Rose switched off her torch and took a wary step towards it. It was a bit tetchy but it wasn't trying to kill them. Maybe it was just lost. Lost and very, very ugly. You couldn't judge by appearances…

'Did you kill all these people here?' Rose asked quickly.

'Don't be absurd,' the creature growled. 'You can see these carcasses are old. The flesh has rotted and there's stuff growing on them.'

Basel swallowed hard. 'So… this ain't your lair, then?'

'A skanky cave like this, my lair?' Faltato twittered, his legs clacking like a pile of bamboo canes toppling over. 'What kind of an animal do you take me for? I come from a world of style and class! I live my life surrounded by art treasures so unutterably beautiful that your puny eyes would implode at the mere sight of them. And you assume my natural habitat to be a rancid rock-hole like this? I was never so insulted – and by bipeds!' The creature whooshed two pincers behind his back and hurled a pile of hardware at their feet. 'Here. You can work these tools.'

Basel looked down at them. 'More construction stuff, from the unit's stores.'

'*I* can't work them,' Rose admitted.

'It was not a statement, it was an instruction,' snapped Faltato. 'You were trying to break through the wall before. The tools will allow you to do this.'

Rose's feeling of unease was growing. 'Why do *you* want to get through there?'

'Because I have a job to do,' said Faltato, puffing up his bulging neck, 'and I have come a very long way in order to do it.'

'You've been sat up in space, polluting the place, haven't you?' she realised.

His five eyes scrunched up in suspicion. 'You detected the ship?'

'In, like, five seconds,' Rose informed him.

'What ship?' hissed Basel.

'Trust me,' Rose murmured, folding her arms and raising her voice. 'So, what were you doing up there?'

Faltato clicked his legs together in a slow, rhythmical manner. 'You will work the tools,' he repeated

Basel jutted out his chin. 'What if we don't?'

He snipped his pincers together. 'Oh, please, let's not go into that.'

'What's on the other side of that wall?' Rose demanded.

'I'm tired of this.' He suddenly surged towards her on his clattering legs, scattering skeletons, all five eyes wide and staring. Then the slash of his mouth opened like a tunnel and something splashed out – long and grey, like a wet vine. It coiled around a skull and threw it into the air. It landed in a dark corner with a clatter.

'I make words with my speaking tongue,' said Faltato. 'I take food – or make points –' he looked at them both meaningfully – 'with my hunting tongue.' His legs vibrated, a sound like a rattlesnake shaking its tail. 'Do not make me show you *other* tongues.'

Rose quickly scooped up one of the tools and looked up at Basel. 'So. Knocking down walls, eh?'

He nodded dubiously. 'How hard can it be?'

Faltato retracted his clay-grey tongue and nodded in approval.

Adiel locked the entrance to the eastern caves, her mind a rushing whirl. She couldn't believe what she had just done to Basel and Rose, couldn't believe that after all these weeks of setting up that everything would kick off tonight. Of course, it would be dangerous. Faced with the prospect of capture and the labour camps, the rebels might well decide to go down fighting.

People could die.

But as she hurried from the entrance she knew she couldn't turn back now. There was so much at stake – not just the villagers' survival, not just the removal of the most brutal militant gang in these parts, but the means to get an official inquiry launched into Fynn's affairs. Let him try to cover up this stuff with the golden blobs – or let this Doctor deal with it on his behalf – Adiel would make sure there was no way Fynn would sweep his involvement with seditious groups under the…

She stumbled to a standstill and her heart seemed to stop with her. There was Fynn now, running towards her, radio clutched in his hand. He knew. Oh, God, he knew, and he was coming to –

'Golems!' The word came out in a strangulated whisper as he almost fell into her arms. 'Main gate, they've all been turned – turned to gold. Like statues, moving statues.'

'What?' Adiel pulled away from him. 'What about security in the grounds?'

'I can't reach anyone!' he shouted. She watched as he made a visible effort to calm himself. 'Have you seen the Doctor or Solomon?'

'No.'

'What about Basel?'

'No,' she insisted, glancing back at the door to the eastern tunnels. 'Now, there must be someone from security who can –'

'There's no one. Those magma forms have left the lava tubes. The golems want to catch us and give us to them.' He gripped hold of her arm. 'We could be the last ones left alive!'

'This can't be happening,' Adiel murmured. 'Not tonight. Not now.' She found herself snatching the radio from his other hand. 'Could this be faulty?'

But he ignored her, staring past her now. 'Oh no,' he said. 'No, no, no…'

Adiel turned to find a grotesque, deformed, golden figure shambling towards them from the direction of the complex. Once it might have been Kanjuchi, but the face was twisted, the body a solid, lumpy mess of muscles, flexing as if they were trying to break through the golden skin that had formed over them.

She pressed the radio to her ear. 'Security, come in please.'

No response.

'Kanjuchi, stay back! It's me, Adiel!'

'He's going to kill us,' Fynn whispered, backing away, pulling her with him. 'Or else make us like he is. We have to hide in the tunnels.'

'No. Not there.'

'We have to!' He started to drag her over, but before they'd covered a couple of metres a loud pounding noise started up from behind the doors. Then a gunshot. And another. 'Who the hell's in there?'

Adiel yanked her arm free, blinked away the tears welling in her eyes, willed away the building static, the nightmare sight of Kanjuchi quickening his step as he stumbled towards them. 'Please!' she shouted into the radio, shouted out into the wide night as she and Fynn ran for cover. 'For God's sake, someone help us!'

NINE

Basel's hands felt half-broken from gripping the demolition tools so hard. They vibrated with energy, sending pulses of power into the thick, dark rock. It was coming away like parts of a scab, but the picking was a slow process. How long before this monster-thing lost its patience and broke *his* skull in a second?

He lowered the pulse tool for a moment, tried to shake the cramp from his arms – and the fog from his head. Most of his life, the big problem had been getting water. Working the pump. Working out each day so he could carry more home the next. Life unchanging, the long hours filled by the numbing routine struggle to survive. He had worked so hard to better himself, to get out into the wider world and see what else life could offer. He'd got an apartment with urban boys, landed a proper job, been listening to the teachers. This morning he'd bounced out of bed as usual, feeling that everything lay ahead of him.

And now here he was, working his guts out in some

secret cave, knee-deep in furry skeletons with some four-armed, five-eyed freak from another planet ready to lick him to death.

It's different, he supposed.

Suddenly Rose powered down her proton hammer.

'Why have you stopped?' enquired Faltato at once, impatiently clip-clopping his skinny hooves on the ground. 'Continue the work.'

'We've only got two hands each,' Rose replied. 'And they're both aching.'

How did she dare to stand up to the thing? Basel felt like he was in a nightmare – one he might never wake up from if this thing was to stick its tongue out at them again.

'The wall is almost penetrated,' said Faltato. 'I am sure of it.'

'Are you?' Rose asked.

The monster sighed. 'Not really. I'm just trying to keep us all motivated.'

Basel picked up the pulse tool again and aimed in at what the sensors assured him was the weakest point. And this time, almost at once, he was rewarded with a thin stream of rock dust showering down from the lumpy ceiling.

'Try there, Rose,' Basel shouted. Maybe then this thing would let them go.

Maybe.

She started up the hammer and blasted at the same point. The stream of dust became a torrent, and then, with a clap of splitting rock, a huge chunk fell away from the wall, cracking and crumbling into the darkness waiting on the other side. Thick dust whooshed into the cavern. Basel choked, tried to draw breath and coughed all the more, felt his eyes streaming.

'I was right!' Faltato shouted. 'My instincts do not desert me! Now, climb up and over into that cave.'

Rose dropped her hammer. 'Why? What's in there?'

'Go and see,' said Faltato. He flicked out his tongue. 'I'll be right behind you.'

Basel swapped an uneasy look with Rose and pulled himself through the hole they'd knocked in the dark, glassy basalt, feeling its hard edges bite into his stomach. Then he swung his legs round and dangled over the edge before dropping down among the rock debris. The swirling dust obscured his view, backlit eerily by the light spilling from Faltato's lamp in the cavern next door. He pulled his torch from his shorts pocket and flicked it on, but only succeeded in turning the thick dust scarlet.

Rose scrambled down beside him, coughing noisily, then flicked on her own torch. 'Come on,' she said. 'He wants something in here, right? If we get it first, we've got something to bargain with.'

'What if he gets *us*?' Basel whispered uneasily. Then in the scarlet smear of the torch beam he caught a gleam of gold.

'It's that stuff!' he shouted. 'That stuff again!'

Next moment, Rose was beside him. 'No,' she said. 'It's *real* gold. Like a little chest or something.' She shone her torch round – and picked out a dark figure looming over them. Basel cowered, but Rose shook her head. 'It's just a statue – stone or something.'

'Stay where you are and touch nothing,' Faltato called to them. Suddenly, a whipcord cracked out from the hole in the rock and wrapped itself round one of the stalactites in the uneven ceiling. It grew taut as a scraping, clattering noise started up.

'Its tongue is a grappling hook,' she whispered.

Basel shuddered, then gave the statue an uneasy second look. He saw now that the shape was tall and sharp like an obelisk but with all these curving fronds rising up from it, like it was having a bad hair day. 'What is it meant to be?'

'They sort of look a bit like wings,' she murmured. 'And see, there's another one over there. Like a bird with its wings… being ripped off.' She smoothed her hands through her hair, uneasy now. 'Not just statues though, look. Paintings and things.'

'Ain't never seen paintings like that before,' Basel murmured. He could see a huge canvas, smeared and scratched with freaky colours he couldn't put names to, birds and planets and abstract shapes he didn't recognise but which somehow sent tingles jarring down his spine. 'How did this stuff get in here, all sealed up?'

'It's a treasure store,' Rose realised. 'Pictures, sculptures…'

'Don't look very African,' said Basel queasily. 'It's alien, right?'

'Right. And if all this was hidden away inside this room, there's got to be another way in and out, yeah? And we've got to find it.'

The ugly cactus head of Faltato peeped into view over

the jagged edge of the demolished wall. A flex of the tongue and two little eyes were glaring at them. Soon he had pulled himself right up, swept his various legs over the side and sat there, staring at them.

'Dunno what you're planning to do with us,' Rose told it fearlessly, 'but check this out. We've got a… a demolishing grenade.' She held up her empty fist like she was clutching something serious. 'If you don't let us go, we'll set it off – blow all this lot to smithereens.'

Faltato's tongue snapped back into his mouth and his blubbery neck rippled. 'I don't believe you,' he said, with smug satisfaction.

Rose shifted her weight awkwardly. 'Well, you'd better.'

He shook his hideous head and pointed with a pincer. 'If you *were* armed, I rather think that guardian would be moving more quickly to envelop you.'

'What?' Basel caught a glimpse of rolling gold movement even as Faltato spoke. 'Oh, God.'

'The blob's back!' Rose joined him in retreating. The thing rolled on towards them, glowing with an oily metallic fire. Basel jumped up on to the base of the statue-obelisk thing and the blob put on speed, surging towards him.

'Excellent,' said Faltato, watching closely.

'Basel, it can climb up, remember?' Rose gestured for him to come back down. 'We'll circle round it, yeah? You go that way, I'll go this.'

He did as she said – and swore as the blob simply split into two so it could bubble after them both.

'Resourceful, isn't it?' Faltato observed.

Rose shot him a poisonous look. 'You just gonna sit there watching while this thing smothers us?'

'That *was* my intention all along,' he admitted.

'Honest, I s'pose,' came a familiar voice from out of the dusty darkness at the rear of the chamber. 'Honest, but nasty.'

Rose's face split open into a mega-grin. 'Doctor!'

He came striding out from the back of the chamber, dodging past a row of angular sculptures, his hair wild, his stare as hard as the basalt. 'Very nasty. Like the suit. By which I don't mean that I *like* the suit – I mean the suit is very nasty. Like you are *also* very nasty, even if you're honest.' He suddenly stopped still, frowning. 'Sorry, everyone, that was a rubbish entrance. Can I go back and start again?'

'Don't you dare,' said Rose. She was obviously dying to run to him, but the blob was blocking her way. It had stopped moving, as if uncertain how to react to this latest arrival. 'Where d'you spring from?'

'Back way in through a hidden tunnel, just found it. Well, just forced it open actually. Solomon knew about this stockpile of tools, right, but the funny thing is that some of them have gone missing. Uh-oh…' He pointed at the speechless Faltato. 'Sorry if I'm jumping to conclusions, but I'm thinking "light-pincers" here. Broke in from the other side, did you? Tut, tut, tut. You're lucky the whole roof hasn't caved in.'

'Who are you?' hissed Faltato, his legs clicking together in agitation.

'Rose gave you a big clue when she called me the Doctor. Oh! Sorry.' He peered at the monster. 'Got any ears? You're gifted in the eye department, I know, but when they were handing out ears…'

'He was front of the queue when they were handing out tongues,' Rose told him. 'Calls himself Faltato, and he's controlling these magma-form things – he has to be.'

'Has he?' The Doctor looked at Faltato. 'Are you?'

'Controlling them?' Faltato was still staring at the blobs, but his middle eye swivelled round to face him. 'Don't be absurd. I'm *observing* them. *Measuring* them.' He made a harsh, rattling sound. 'Much as you are, I imagine.'

The Doctor smiled. 'Big room chock-full of Valnaxi art treasures and here you are, watching the guard dogs.'

'So you know of the Valnaxi,' Faltato said darkly.

'Who doesn't? Avian race, gifted artists. Gifted telepaths too – seems they actually connected with their own planet.'

Rose frowned. 'What, the planet had a brain or something?'

'It had a spirit! A buzz! A passion all its own.' The Doctor flung out his arms. 'It was their muse, it inspired them, helped them create the most amazing, beautiful – beeeee-*yoo*-tiful – art. Their stuff goes for a bomb. But it was bombs that did for the Valnaxi.' He glanced between Basel and Rose. 'Got caught up in this really awful war, see. They held on to their planet for as long as they could –'

'And then they were crushed,' Faltato concluded.

'The winning side always writes their version of history,' said the Doctor. 'They had time to build all this. Doesn't sound like a crushed race to me.'

Basel frowned. 'What you on about?'

'These blobs of magma, yeah? They *are* sentries, just like I thought, guarding this little hoard! Oh, but not just guarding it. *Protecting* it.' He nodded at Faltato. 'I was right about the light-pincers, wasn't I? You're a thief! Oooh, yes. A dirty great tea-leaf!'

'You talk a lot,' Faltato complained.

'Can talk the hind legs off a donkey,' the Doctor agreed, 'but where would I start with you, eh?'

'Why have the blobs stopped?' Rose hissed.

'The guardians recognise they are in the presence of aliens,' Faltato said. 'They are assessing the risks we each pose and formulating a strategy of how best to deal with us. From the time it's taking them, there's clearly significant degradation in the central circuitry…'

Suddenly the blobs started rolling towards the Doctor with horrible speed.

'Doctor!' yelled Rose.

The blobs converged, became a superblob and surged hungrily onwards. The Doctor hurled himself to one side. 'Solomon, now!' The superblob made no attempt to follow him, sticking to its course.

Solomon? Basel stared into the gloom at the back of the cavern, just as a bristling haze of green light snapped from out of there and fixed on to the superblob, making it ripple like molten gold jelly. The ground started to shake as if in sympathy.

'All right, kill the power!' the Doctor called.

The green light duly faded and Solomon came edging nervously into view, staring round at the room's weird wonders and gripping an electro-masher in both hands – a tool more often used for smashing up concrete. He must have been hiding back there with the Doctor. 'Did I kill *that* thing?'

'Of course you didn't,' snapped Faltato. 'But I'm grateful to you for the demonstration.'

'What... is that?' Solomon swung up the masher to cover the creature on the wall. In a second, Faltato's tongue had whipped out like one of Spider-Man's webs, wrapped itself around the end of the tube and yanked it out of Solomon's hands.

The Doctor glared at him. 'Thought I told you to stay out of sight?'

"S all right, man,' said Basel, rushing over to his boss's side. '*I'm* glad to see you!'

'What's happening here?' Solomon breathed, staring between his empty hands and the thing on the wall. 'Special effects? They making a movie down here?'

'Disaster movie, maybe,' Rose muttered.

Faltato studied the masher briefly, then casually dropped it behind him, back into the chamber of bones. Then he sucked in his tongue like a thick string of very nasty spaghetti, pincers clicking open and closed, rapt in concentration. 'Come on... Any moment now...'

The blob flared into sudden brightness. It started rolling slowly towards Solomon. As if it wanted revenge.

'Recovered from sonic disruption within twelve

chrono-ticks,' Faltato noted. 'Taken together with the delay in strategy formulation, overall degradation of performance would suggest to me that these guardians have lain dormant for maybe… 2,000 years, local time?' He threw his head back and made a vile, spluttering, sniggering sound. 'Yes!' he crowed, clapping all four pincers together. 'The age matches up. This is the last Valnaxi art warren. The final burial ground for all the finest treasures.'

'Speaking of burial grounds…' Rose pointed to the magma blob. It was glowing brighter, surging forwards.

'Out of here,' the Doctor snapped, grabbing Rose by the hand. 'Run!'

Solomon was first to turn and sprint for it, leading Basel to the narrow fissure in the rock that was almost invisible in the shadows. He didn't look back.

'Where we going now?' Basel asked shakily.

'Through there is a side tunnel,' the Doctor told him, 'joins on to the central lava tube. But watch your step. I don't think it's too stable.'

'Right now, don't think I am,' said Rose weakly.

'Did you see the bones?' Basel asked him.

The Doctor frowned. 'What bones?'

'There's a load of old skeletons in the cave next door,' Rose put in.

'Well, unless you want to get ours added to the pile – shift! Basel, you first.'

Basel pushed through the split in the volcanic stone, ran hell for leather down the winding tunnel, his red torch lighting the way, until finally he saw the opening that led on to the central lava tube.

And found Solomon looking down the wrong end of a plasma rifle wielded by a young kid with scared, staring eyes. He was flanked by two older guys, all bullet belts and bandanas.

Adiel's rebels, thought Basel, terrified as one of the men shoved a rifle in his face. *Now we're really gonna get it.*

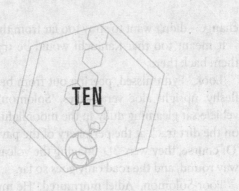

TEN

Adiel was running through the darkened crop field, Fynn just ahead of her. With all doors to the unit guarded by golems, with the eastern tunnels overrun by the scum of the earth and with Kanjuchi's new friends blocking off the main gate and the entrance to the western growth chambers, there was literally nowhere else to go – nowhere that afforded them cover.

The lava tubes probably weren't such a good idea anyway, since they had spawned the magma forms. And if she ran into the rebels there, what would she say – 'Sorry, would you mind coming back to pillage and kill later on when we've got reinforcements ready to ambush you please?'

The big scheme, so long in the planning, had gone to hell. And in turn a piece of hell had come here to get them. Every time she and Fynn paused for breath she heard the sound of the Kanjuchi golem crashing through the crop towards them. Presumably that meant that the magma form itself – the stuff that actually performed the change – didn't want to stray too far from the lava tubes.

It meant too that Kanjuchi would be trying to herd them back there.

'Look,' Fynn hissed, peering out from between some fleshy, upright aloe vera leaves. 'Solomon's jeep!' The vehicle sat gleaming dully in the moonlight, abandoned on the dirt track at the periphery of the paved walkway. 'Of course, they were 3D-imaging the volcano, right the way round, and the road only goes so far.'

'Poor Solomon,' Adiel murmured. 'He must have not wanted to drive on the walkways.'

'It's not permitted,' Fynn agreed. 'But they might have got inside the eastern tunnels on foot. It might have been *them* we heard behind the door!'

Or else the rebels have found them, Adiel realised, her head pounding.

The dull throb was echoed by the thump of Kanjuchi's progress through the fields, getting ever louder. He was closing on them fast.

'Keys are still in the ignition,' Fynn noted. 'Maybe we could ram through the perimeter fence, get help.'

Adiel nodded, broke cover from the borders of the crop field and jumped into the passenger seat. Fynn climbed up into the driver's seat, his gaunt face beaded with sweat. In all the years since she'd left Moundou, Adiel had never once imagined that her survival might somehow depend on Director Fynn.

The other way around, perhaps…

He turned the ignition key. The engine grumped into life. Then he gripped hold of the steering wheel as if psyching himself up for what would come next.

It came sooner than they could have guessed. Suddenly, the bloated, gleaming monster that Kanjuchi had become came crashing out of the crops towards them, dredging a roar from the depths of his golden throat.

Rose wriggled out through the narrow fissure after the Doctor. The blob was still coming.

'See if I can close the door behind us...' He started sonicking at the wall.

Rose waited tensely. 'So these Valnaxi – they're meant to be good with a paintbrush, yeah?'

'That's like saying Da Vinci was OK at drawing,' the Doctor retorted. 'The Valnaxi race produced more gifted artists than you'd think was possible. A very attuned people, very spiritual... At least they were, before the war.'

'Sent them barmy, did it?'

'No good,' he murmured. 'Can't get the frequency. Come on!' They moved along the tunnel after Basel and Solomon. 'What d'you mean, "barmy"?'

'Well, why would anyone bury their art treasures in a volcano, let alone a volcano on another planet?'

'Good hiding place,' he explained. 'Makes sense when there's a war on. Take your lot. Second World War, bombs dropping over London, you don't want all your best pictures and sculptures going up in smoke, do you? So you evacuate them to the countryside! You hide them in castle dungeons, or lock them up in prisons.' He stopped and smiled as if recalling some fond memory. 'The National Gallery shoved everything they had under a mountain in North Wales. The trouble we had getting *Charles I on Horseback* under Ffestiniog Bridge! Mind you, that was nothing compared to hoicking the *Mona Lisa* up Everest in the fifty-first century – on a camel...'

'So these Valnaxi,' Rose said in an effort to get back on-topic, 'did they dump all their art on Earth?'

'Shouldn't think so. Probably got treasures salted away in backwaters all over the galaxy. Earth was certainly nice and quiet 2,000 years ago. Poor old Valnaxi weren't to know what a nuisance its people would grow up to be, how much attention they'd attract...' They had reached the hole in the rock which led to the main tunnel. 'Not to mention just how much trouble –'

'– they'd get into?' Rose concluded, pushing through the hole and, in a moment of sharp, sudden horror, taking in the sight of Solomon and Basel being held by three men at gunpoint.

'Westerners,' said the oldest of the men. 'Could be worth a bit.' He jabbed his gun against Solomon's neck and sneered at her. 'Any more of you in there?'

Rose shook her head dumbly. You sort of expected the weird cactus-crab stuff with the Doctor, but *this*... this was a terror closer to home.

Luckily the Doctor seemed less fazed. 'Hello!' He grinned as he took in the three armed figures. 'You know, I thought I heard movement in the tunnels as we came along here before. We must have just missed each other! Imagine that. It's like a farce, a French farce. Have you met the French, by the way?'

The tall man, clearly the leader, raised his automatic weapon at the Doctor in warning. 'We went into the grounds of your unit, but the door's locked. We came down here looking for another way to get inside.' He grinned. 'Looks like we found it.'

The Doctor sighed wearily. 'You wanna know how much time we have for this?'

'Give us trouble, we waste all of you.' The teen gripped hold of Basel's arm. 'We don't need you – none of you. Our men are still down there. They'll force that door open in the end.'

Solomon closed his eyes. 'So they can take all the food they like and murder anyone who gets in their way?'

'If they have to.' The leader shrugged. 'What do we owe state-lovers like you?'

'"Scuse me,' the Doctor piped up. 'Little matter of killer alien blob coming down the tunnel behind us –'

The leader swung his gun up into the Doctor's face. 'Another word out of you and –'

'Oh! Ta very much,' said the Doctor, whipping the weapon away. 'But I don't think that'll be much use blocking this hole.' He chucked it casually through the split in the stone. 'Nope, no use at all.'

The teen gawped at what the Doctor had done – and Solomon grabbed hold of his gun barrel. As the two of them wrestled with the machine gun, it went off, firing up at the rocky ceiling. The noise was incredible, a hundred times nastier than the muted rattle you heard in films or on the news. Rose's ears rang as stinging shards of shrapnel burst from the stone like hail from a storm cloud, sending everyone staggering back.

'Shut that up!' the Doctor yelled at the third man, yanking the gun away and shoving it brusquely into Solomon's arms. 'Keep them covered. I can't hear myself think!' He had the sonic screwdriver in his hand. 'Honestly! We've got to seal up that hole – have you any idea how difficult it is to resonate sound frequencies through rock this thick when…'

'Look out!' Rose shouted as the roof began to fall down.

'Oh,' said the Doctor, springing back from the downpour of pebbles and dust. 'Well, I suppose firing forty rounds a second into a fault line and starting a rock fall might *also* do the job.'

Rose grabbed him by the hand and pulled him clear as the main tunnel caved in and the opening vanished behind tons of rock. As the echoes crashed round the passageway like explosions, Rose covered her head and hoped for the best.

The best actually turned out to be being knocked off her feet by what felt like a miniature earthquake and ending up on the ground with her head squashed between Basel's legs. She pulled herself free and found the Doctor just beside her, staring urgently back down the dust-clouded passage. The three men had scrambled away along the tunnel, their frightened shouts carrying in loose, hollow echoes.

The Doctor beamed. 'Well, that seems to have worked out OK!'

'Yeah?' Rose pointed ahead of them.

Through the thick, spiralling dust, maybe five metres away, dozens of tiny glowing lights were crawling sluggishly towards them like drunken fireflies.

'That guardian creature's squeezed through the rock fall in globules.' The Doctor was already scrambling to his feet. 'But it's gonna coalesce. Quick, before it pulls itself together.'

'Me,' Solomon murmured, staring at the pulsing little lights like he was hypnotised. 'It wants *me*.'

'Don't get big-headed, now,' the Doctor chided, ushering all of them back. 'It'll settle for any or all of us.'

'Where can we go?' Basel asked, backing away still further. 'That cave-in didn't just block the side tunnel. There's no way back to the agri-unit.'

Solomon stirred at the news, swung round, his face unreadable. 'No way of getting any more food for the village.'

Rose felt a chill go through her as the little points of light on the cave floor began to merge into one. 'Doctor, where *are* we gonna go?'

'Can't make for the village,' said Basel grimly. 'Them with the guns could be getting reinforcements. Or waiting to take us out.'

'Ooh! Nice trip to the pictures? Lovely.' The Doctor had pulled a small monitor screen from his trouser pocket. 'Luckily I brought my A–Z with me. Guide to the whole lava-tube network and its contents. It's how we found you.' He nodded proudly. 'Oh yeah, it's all here, you know – points of historical interest and artistic merit, secret treasure troves from distant planets – that place we were in was one of at least three adjoining caverns chock-full of Valnaxi artworks...' He smiled at Rose as if they were about to take a stroll in a country garden. 'Turns out that these caves are regular Aladdin's... um, caves.'

The guardian was still a few metres away, but it was pulsing now with a deep golden light, like a metallic heart thumping away on the floor.

'Wherever we're going, how about we get started?' Basel shouted.

'We'll have to take a new route.' The Doctor was staring at the screen. 'Keep cutting through the chambers until we find a way back outside – and see what clues we can pick up on the way.'

'Clues?' said Solomon, frowning.

'Don't you wanna know what's going on round here?' the Doctor asked, looking genuinely surprised. 'I mean, funny-looking alien, ancient treasures hidden under a mountain, golden blobs blobbing all over the place and spaceship exhaust fumes in the upper atmosphere... Dunno about you, but my interest is piqued.'

'Well, don't pique too soon,' Rose warned him, backing away as the guardian lurched towards them, rolling like a big glowing football. 'Looks like that thing's getting its act together.'

'Right then!' He crouched down and started feeling around the rock on the right of the passage.

'Better move it, Doctor,' whispered Basel.

A rustling, chittering, scrabbling noise had started up

behind them, slowly swelling in volume.

'Bats,' Rose breathed.

A chorus of screams went up and she shuddered. Sounded like the rebels had found a way out of sorts. A golden glow was starting to creep in the dark stretch of tunnel.

The Doctor fiddled with the sonic screwdriver. With a thundering roar, a split zigzagged up through the dark rock. 'Everyone through!' he cried. 'C'mon!'

Adiel shrieked as the lumpy, deformed image of Kanjuchi came pelting towards them.

'Hang on!' Fynn shouted. He stamped on the accelerator. With a frightened squeal of tyres, the jeep lunged forwards and mounted the paved area.

'Can we run the main gates?' Adiel wondered. 'If we can get up enough speed, ram them head on…'

As they passed the entrance to the eastern network, she saw with a sick feeling that the door was standing wide open.

'Solomon and the Doctor,' said Fynn, slewing to a stop. 'They must have got out.'

'Transport!' screamed a stranger's voice. 'Quick!'

Suddenly two men in filthy, stained fatigues came out from the mouth of the doorway, carrying a third man between them whose body looked to be solid gold.

'They think they can save him,' Adiel realised.

'Who the hell are they?' Fynn roared.

But before Adiel could answer, a fourth figure appeared from the mouth of the tunnels and aimed a rifle at them. 'Get out!' he screamed. 'We need your transport!'

Fynn stuck the jeep into first gear and floored the accelerator. 'Down, Adiel!' he shouted as the jeep skidded away – and as the rebel opened fire.

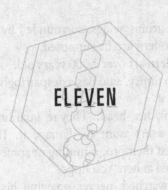

ELEVEN

Solomon stared round at his surroundings in trepidation, still clutching the guerrilla's gun tight in his sweating hands. He, Basel and the girl had followed the Doctor into another large, vaulted chamber like the one Faltato had forced them to open – only this one was filled with even more abstract, unfathomable objects in stone and metal.

The Doctor was over at the far wall, tapping the rock with his screwdriver thing. 'Try to block off the entrance,' he shouted.

Basel stared at him hopelessly. 'What with?'

'One of the paintings or something.'

'But the bats can fly in over it!' Solomon protested.

The Doctor didn't look up. 'So make it a *big* painting.'

Basel made straight for the largest canvas he could find and Rose rushed over to give him a hand. Solomon went up to one of the paintings himself and found it wasn't canvas at all – it was something sticky, like spider's webs squashed together, and showed some skinny thing with wide, wide burning wings, surrounded by curvy white squiggles. Modern art, he supposed.

Yeah. Modern art over 2,000 years old.

'This is too flimsy,' said Basel despairingly. 'They'll just tear through it.'

Rose shook her head. 'They're guarding this stuff, yeah? They won't want to damage it. That'd be… I dunno, against their programming or something.'

Basel looked at her. 'You hope.'

Solomon watched, nerves gnawing his stomach as together they put the painting in position. But it didn't cover the whole of the split. The rush and flutter of the bats was loud and still rising. It was almost like it was inside his head. Solomon shut his eyes, wished he could just hide somewhere. Somewhere safe.

'What we gonna do?' Basel shouted.

Solomon opened his eyes and hoped his mouth would follow suit, that wise, calming words would magically come.

But the only things coming were the bats, and when Solomon's mouth *did* open, it was to scream. The misshapen creatures swooped into the massive chamber, burning fiery bright. Rose and Basel clung on to each other, then sprinted to join the Doctor. Without hesitation, the bats bunched together like a heavy golden cloud – over Solomon.

'No!' he screamed, and opened fire with the battered gun. The recoil nearly twisted the weapon from his hands. He gripped it as if he was trying to throttle it, gasped as the red blasts of light pumped from the barrel.

Some of the bats jerked in mid-air, smashed together as they took direct hits. One spiralled down, out of control, taking the top off a weird, looping stone sculpture. Its agonised screech rose above the raucous racket, as if the damage done to the art was a hundred times worse than anything a bullet could do.

Then the gun jerked dead in Solomon's hands. 'I'm out of bullets!' he yelled – as the bats finally swooped down on him.

He felt the gun beaten from his hands by jostling wings and claws, felt the weight of their burning gold bodies pressing in, smothering. He fell to his knees. His ears rang with their inhuman screeching as claws scraped against his eyes, wings gouged at his skin, twitching heads pushed into his mouth...

As dark alien thoughts scorched away his own.

'We've got to help him,' Rose gasped, watching as Solomon flailed around beneath the seething golden mass.

'Five more seconds,' said the Doctor tersely.

Basel ran to his boss. He tried to scoop up the bats in his fists, throw them clear, but every time he dragged one away it flapped straight back to join the smothering mass. Rose pitched in, flailing at them with her fists. But one flapped straight into her face, golden teeth bared, and another started clawing at her hair, driving her back. She heard an ear-splitting clap as the Doctor's work ripped open the rock.

Then, as she turned, she saw the Doctor charging over,

sonic raised, fiddling with the settings as he went. He waved it like a magic wand over the seething, glowing bustle of life and suddenly the creatures started falling away, shrieking and streaming up to the high ceiling. Solomon burst from the golden cocoon terrified, covered in welts and scratches – but alive. Basel put an arm round him, helped to keep him standing as he started to shiver with shock.

'Why didn't they kill him?' Rose asked.

'They were trying to,' Basel argued.

The Doctor looked at Solomon almost accusingly. 'Or else they want him for something.'

'Couldn't breathe,' Solomon whispered, leaning on Basel for support.

Rose looked up warily at the bats. 'What did you do to them, Doctor?'

'Remember the way we gave the Krillitanes a headache in that school with the fire alarm?' He shrugged. 'There's enough bat left in these poor little loves not to like ultra-high frequencies. Caught them by surprise.' He ran over to the zigzag split he had made in the cavern wall. 'But we may not be so lucky a second time, so *shift*!'

Rose helped Basel half-carry, half-drag Solomon through to what she hoped was safety. Not a chance. The cavern was near identical in size, but filled with a different type of art – huge crystal display cases full of weird clay dishes and cups with loads of handles.

'Those bat things will just come straight through into here,' sighed Basel, helping Solomon to sit down on the floor.

124

'Rose, Basel, move a display case up against the split,' the Doctor told them.

They did as he asked, for what it was worth. Then they helped Solomon over to join the Doctor, who was working at the right-hand wall. It gleamed in the red torchlight like a mirror of dark glassy rock.

'Can't you use your magic stick to seal the rock back up again?' Basel asked.

'It's not a magic stick,' said the Doctor, consulting his little screen. 'All it's doing is opening the in-built doors. Valnaxi tools hollowed out these chambers when the lava tubes were fresh-formed, keeping them safe from further eruptions. And they left mechanisms behind in the rock so they could open them again some day.' He started tapping the wall with his fingers. 'Basel, stand sentry at the crack in the wall. Shout if you see anything we should know about.'

Basel nodded, slunk away.

'And you, Solomon – try to get your strength back, big feller.' The Doctor nodded to himself. 'I think you're gonna need it.'

Solomon sat down heavily, looking totally lost in this alien place.

Rose sighed. 'So each one of these caverns is like a safe, yeah?'

'A safe within a safe, within a safe. So you need a good alarm system, right? Something that can detect possible intruders at long-range. And how would you do that?'

'Sniff out spaceship pollution in the atmosphere,' Rose realised. '*Faltato*'s spaceship.'

'That woke it up, put it on stand-by,' the Doctor agreed.

'And then Fynn's boys excavating the tunnels was like a burglar going to work on the safe with dynamite,' Rose realised. 'Set off the alarms, woke up the magma.'

'Nice analogy. And I reckon we really *do* have a burglar about – Faltato.' The Doctor scowled. 'I get the feeling he knows something we don't. I mean *apart* from what it's like to wear pants with fifty leg-holes. He was observing the guardians, measuring their reflexes. What's he up to? Eh?'

'Whatever, he must be happy we're making our getaway through here,' Rose remarked.

He frowned. 'How d'you mean?'

'Well, we're cracking all the safes for him, aren't we?' As if to prove her point, the rock-face burst open with the now familiar but no less deafening CRUMP and they both choked on the thick dust. 'Funny. Why isn't he coming after us?'

'I'll tell you something else that's a bit odd,' said the Doctor. 'This is the deepest safe, the priciest stuff should be here – makes sense, right? So how come there are no guardians sealed up with them, waiting to bite intruders on the leg?'

'It's quiet out there,' Basel called across, his voice echoing round the chamber. 'Dead quiet.'

'Why would they just give up?' Rose wondered, before inspiration struck. 'Maybe you scared them. Or maybe they know you're not the real bad guy in this – I mean, it's not like you're really breaking in, is it? You're using the sonic as a sort of spare key to *let* you in.'

The Doctor didn't sound convinced. 'Or maybe the guardians are waiting – working to some kind of a plan, like Faltato.' He peered into the soupy gloom of the next cavern. 'Question is, what?'

'That's *your* question,' said Rose briskly. 'Mine is, where did that room full of mouldy old skeletons come from?' A shiver ran through her. 'And how far do we have to go through these caves until we reach an exit?'

'That's two questions. Cheat.' The Doctor squinted at the screen. 'But looking at the A–Z, there's a proper little rabbit's warren of lava tubes the other side of this cave, leading west. Should take us out near where Kanjuchi struck gold in the first place…'

'And where that vulture made a hole in the wall,' Rose recalled.

'We can't go back there,' said Solomon fervently.

'It's the only way,' the Doctor told him.

'The vulture, though,' said Rose. 'Why *did* it make that hole? Surely this smart-magma stuff would want to make the place more secure, not less.'

'Doesn't seem to be any art stored there – but I think that chamber must be something a bit special.' The Doctor's eyes had lost their sparkle, turned stern and serious. 'When the systems were activated, the magma needed more guards – it had to get out there, recruiting golems for the cause, and it wanted them to be able to get into those caves…' He pressed his tongue against his teeth and blew out a whistling breath. 'You know, it's a shame about Fynn. I really think he *did* want to save the world. Instead, his little agri-unit here might just be the place that's gonna destroy it.'

Adiel heard nothing but the gunshots, wondering which one would hit, wondering how quickly she'd die. Fynn accelerated, sending the growl of the engine into a frantic roar. They bumped off the paved concourse on to a bark-chipped pathway, then on to the dirt track. Adiel kept her head down, felt the wind whipping her long braids behind her as Fynn hurled the jeep from side to side – sharp, panicking tugs on the wheel that threatened to tip her out. If the bullets didn't kill her, a fall at this speed surely would. And if she wasn't killed outright, the magma forms would simply roll along and take her for themselves, lay their golden shroud over her skin…

'I think we're out of range,' Fynn shouted, his voice like a fist knocking her back to the moment.

She fumbled with the seat belt, clicked it home with trembling hands.

'Fynn!' one of the rebels screamed after them. 'Damn it, Fynn, come back here, you son of a…'

The roar of the engine drowned him out. 'He recognised you, knew your name,' Adiel realised.

'I… I'm Director here,' Fynn blustered. 'Of course he knows *of* me.'

'Let's just run the main gate,' she said shakily, not daring to raise her head.

'We've gone past it,' said Fynn. 'Too many golems. Not just the guards but dogs and hyenas too – all the wildlife round the volcano's fair game for this force. We'd never make it through.' He shook his head angrily. 'We need troops. We need help here or we're going to lose everything. Everything.'

'I didn't think I had much left to lose,' Adiel said, looking down at her clenched fists. Her knuckles were showing pale through her dark skin, like little eyes staring back at her. 'Not since I lost my parents in Moundou, to scum like those men back there.' She paused. 'Men you were seen consorting with around that time,' she added quietly.

He didn't answer, and some sudden instinct made her look up – just in time to see two massive, hunched-up golems come shambling out from behind the main complex to block their path. In a second she recognised one of them from the security patrol. He'd always smiled at her when she left each evening – she'd never even bothered to learn his name. That friendly smile was twisted now into an insane grimace. Beside him was someone she didn't know. Had to be a rebel. She'd been planning to get Smiley to help capture the likes of him – now here they were working together to ambush her.

'No!' she screamed, as Fynn kept driving straight for them. They didn't attempt to move clear. It was like hitting two trees in quick succession. The impact knocked the golems metres into the air and sent the jeep careening out of control.

Time seemed to slow. Fynn screamed as the jeep spun round in a large circle. Adiel saw the huge pile of metal canisters stacked up beside a storehouse – *what the hell are they doing there?* – and realised with a crushing sense of inevitability that they would hit –

The collision sounded like metal thunder, a ringing and clanging as if hell's bells were tolling. The canisters tumbled down over the jeep. One struck her on the back of her head, blotting out everything except thick, searing pain. Though the jeep had finally shuddered to a stop, her vision was spinning faster than ever.

'Adiel?' Fynn gasped. 'We have to get out of here.' He was turning the ignition key but the engine wasn't biting. 'Right now.'

She squinted ahead into the pool of fierce light cast by the headlamps. It was as if a golden stream had opened up in the ground ahead of them, writhing with movement. 'What's that?' she asked sluggishly, tasting blood at the back of her throat.

'I think they're ants,' Fynn hissed. He was yanking at her seat belt, trying to release it. 'Driver ants, a whole colony.' He strained with the belt but it was jammed. 'We're right in their way. Even if they weren't golems, they could tear us to pieces!'

Faltato hauled himself back through the cave of human bones, along the narrow passage, towards the little hole he'd made in the rock-fall and finally out into the main tunnel. He was glad his brothers in the Hadropilatic Fellowship could not see him now. Many of them would have killed to see him on his knees in old excrement – and committed wholesale slaughter if it had been fresh.

Simple jealousy, he told himself. *They don't have your drive. They don't have your skills.*

They certainly didn't have his debts, the swines.

He produced a meso-sensor from the moneybelt around his midriff and clacked away down the tunnel. The appearance of this presumptuous Doctor bothered him. Clearly, he was some sort of expert agent, and surely his agenda must be similar – but for whom was he working?

Well, no matter. He could be dealt with in due course. Bipeds were notoriously fragile creatures. They broke so easily.

If only the same were not true of these rock formations – the tunnel network must be close to tumbling down around their ears. It had pained him to use heavy-duty construction tools under such circumstances. If he found the *Lona Venus*, only to crush it beneath tons of rock…

He'd never hear the end of it at home. Assuming he survived long enough to make it back…

Now he had assessed the guardians' circuit degradation and estimated their activation date, and was certain this *was* the last remaining Valnaxi art warren, he simply needed to locate the security plaque and his work here was done. But something was niggling at him. The behaviour of the guardians was absolutely consistent with those he had encountered before while breaking warrens, except…

He frowned. It was almost *too* consistent. As if these guardians were putting on an act for him. As if there was more to them than met the eyes…

Picking his way over a particularly large mound of

fallen rock, Faltato became aware of a dim, golden glow. There was a hole in the roof, through which he could see the unfamiliar stars in their scattergun patterns, and the distant diamond of the ship hovering in orbit. But that didn't explain why his hooves were gleaming orange.

He slapped the meso-sensor with one pincer and it pinged importantly. Faltato looked down as the glow rose dimly to warm the dark cracks. He was standing *on top of* the security plaque.

And it was buried beneath tons of rock.

'Oh, well. I've done all I can,' he consoled himself, flicking his tongue out through the hole in the roof. Once he'd secured it around a stone projectile, he started to winch himself up, clicking all four pincers together in anticipation.

It was time to guide down his sponsors.

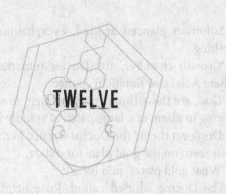

TWELVE

Rose wondered if she would ever see daylight again, or if she'd have crimson vision for evermore. She was exhausted, jumpy through lack of sleep. The passage was snaking on and on endlessly, uncomfortably cramped and narrow. She, Basel and Solomon trooped along in silence, the Doctor leading the way.

'Hello,' he said, stopping abruptly. A hole about the size of a chubby Labrador had been made in the side of the wall. 'What d'you think made that, then?'

'Fat mutant mouse?' Rose suggested.

'Very helpful mouse.' The Doctor checked his gadget. 'Because this hole is exactly where we need one to be.'

'Coincidence,' said Rose uneasily.

The Doctor got down on all fours and shuffled through the gap. Basel helped Solomon, who was still in a total daze since his ordeal with the bats.

'Oh yes.' The Doctor looked all round. 'Remember this, Solomon? Seems like only yesterday. It *was* only yesterday.'

Solomon glanced around, eyes haunted, but said nothing.

'Growth chamber,' the Doctor remarked. 'The one where Adiel saw Kanjuchi change.'

'God, are these things mushrooms?' Rose wondered, staring in alarm at a large patch of spindly fungus.

'Don't eat them,' the Doctor warned her. 'You'd break your teeth on the gold plate for a start…'

'What gold plate?' said Basel.

The Doctor whirled round. Rose helpfully pointed her torch at the 'shrooms. 'Hang on,' he said. 'When I came here with Fynn, these were golem-mushrooms. Now they're back to normal again.' He snapped one off at the stalk. 'The DNA of the original has reverted.'

Solomon seemed to stir a little at this. 'How come fungus can do that but people can't?'

'Dunno. Simpler life form maybe? Or maybe the magma realised that mushrooms aren't exactly the scariest soldiers in the world and wrote them off as a bad idea.' The Doctor shrugged. 'Speaking of bad ideas, I want to check out the back of this cave.'

He set off cautiously – just as the growth chamber lit up like a Catherine wheel.

'Doctor!' Rose yelled, her insides twisting.

A guardian had surged through the mutant mousehole, huge and undulating, glowing as if white-hot. Basel backed away alongside Rose – but Solomon just stood there.

The blob rolled forwards towards him.

'Everyone keep back!' the Doctor yelled, ignoring his

own advice as he ran to drag Solomon clear.

Too late.

With a sudden spurt of speed, the blob elongated and squelched itself around Solomon's hand. Solomon shrieked with pain as in a matter of seconds he was sucked into its swelling, pulsing mass. Then just as quickly the blob retreated back through its hole.

'What do we do?' Basel shouted, wild-eyed and anguished.

'We get after them,' said the Doctor, already running for the hole.

But as he neared it, a gleaming creature the size of a cat scuttled out on warped, knotted legs. Rose was almost sick. Once, this thing had been a scorpion. Now it was a nightmare monster, waving its crusty gold claws in warning, flexing its hideous golden sting high over its head. Another one was jostling to get out just behind it, scratching its sting against the rock.

The Doctor looked back at Rose and the others. 'No sudden moves,' he warned them.

'You gotta be kidding me!' Basel whispered as a huge gleaming spider came clacking out of the adjoining cave, its heavy legs quivering as it dragged its bloated body across the floor towards them, its many eyes a dark molten gold.

'Change of plan!' the Doctor cried airily. 'Sudden moves, anyone?' He trampled mushrooms in his dash to reach the far side of the growth chamber, made a stirrup with his hands. 'Vulture hole in the wall up there. Don't stop till you're safely through it.'

Basel wiped sweat from his eyes, or maybe tears. 'What about Solomon?'

The spider's mandibles twitched disgustingly as it skittered forwards. The two scorpions crept out to reveal a third just behind them. 'Move,' the Doctor insisted.

Basel pushed up on the Doctor's stirrup and started to scale the wall.

'Is there nothing we can do for Solomon?' Rose said quietly, plonking her own dirty trainer into his palms.

'Stay alive,' he said, 'and hope things can change.'

The scorpions kept stalking towards them, claws scissoring open and shut. The Doctor and Rose climbed quickly after Basel.

Adiel watched Fynn as he struggled to free her from the seat belt, as the mass of giant driver ants marched ever nearer.

'Why don't you just get out of here!' she shouted.

He only shook his head.

'But they're almost on us!'

Her skin crawled. She knew what they did. If you were in their way they would climb under your clothing and attack you *en masse*, biting into your flesh with their heavy jaws and pulling backwards until chunks came away. She had seen doctors in the village stitch wounds with the ants when sutures were in short supply. Once those jaws dug into your flesh, nothing could prise them loose – even if you squeezed off the ant's head, they would stay locked tight there.

'It's no good,' he gasped.

The ants had reached the jeep now. Adiel struggled, her head throbbing, panting for breath.

But they didn't attack. They just swarmed past.

Finally, with a ratcheting sound like harsh laughter, the seat belt came free. Adiel twisted round and watched the hideous procession bustle past.

'Thanks,' she said distantly.

'Looks like they've got somewhere to go,' Fynn muttered.

Then Adiel jumped as a rushing, screeching, chattering sound exploded into the air. Bats were swarming out from the foothills of Mount Tarsus. Thousands of them. The air thickened with tiny gleaming bodies as they gathered to blot out the moon and the stars.

'Them too,' she murmured. 'What's happening?'

She craned her neck to follow their flight – till her eyes came to rest on a dark, unshaven face. Her body jolted with surprise. The man wore a turban over a soldier's helmet, carried a gun, clamped a dirty hand over her mouth to stop her screaming.

'So you stopped for us in the end, Fynn, huh?' He smiled to reveal a mouth struck with golden teeth. His friend stood behind him, trying to support the gleaming statue of their comrade. 'I don't know what the hell is happening here, but you know science. You're going to help Mula here.'

Fynn shook his head. 'No one can help this man.'

Adiel pulled her face free, stared up at Fynn defiantly.

'Won't you introduce me, Director?'

'*Director* Fynn may not remember me. My name is Guwe.' The man with the golden teeth smiled again. 'But perhaps you'll remember Isako, huh? He asked me to send you his finest regards.'

Roba Isako. Chad's Most Wanted.

'So, Roba put you up to this,' Fynn sneered. 'Is he your president today, your king perhaps? What's your little band called this week – the Free Chad Alliance? Enclave of Liberty, Brothers of Chad Militia…'

Guwe raised his gun – when with a harsh, splintering, snapping sound Mula's skinny golden body suddenly writhed and fattened as if it was filling with water. One grotesquely swollen arm lashed out and struck the man who was supporting him in the throat. The rebel's head snapped back and stayed there, as if he was watching the stars, till his legs gave way and he crashed lifeless to the floor.

'Mula, no!' Guwe shouted, but the golem was already pounding away into the night, as if trying to catch up with the ants and the bats. All three of them watched him go, united in shock. 'What the hell's happening here?' Guwe checked his friend's prone body, then rose and rounded angrily on Fynn. 'What's happened to Mula? What did you do?'

'I'm not responsible for any of this –'

'Listen,' said Adiel, looking about. 'So quiet.'

Guwe nodded slowly. 'None of the sounds of night.'

'Every animal has been taken,' Fynn murmured. 'And now they're answering a call we can't hear.'

Adiel was barely listening. A vivid blue light was slowly pulsing where foothills ended and night sky began. 'What's that?'

'The thing that scared the golems away?' Fynn wondered.

'We're not staying to find out,' Guwe insisted, covering them both with the gun. 'We need shelter – so *move.*'

'Look at them,' breathed Rose.

She and the Doctor had made it out through the hole and joined Basel, grateful that the monster spiders and scorpions seemed to be staying down there to guard the place.

But they were about the only ones.

Rose, Basel and the Doctor stood close together in silence, staring out over the grounds of the agri-unit. From here, high up in the foothills, Rose could see that all golems great and small had gathered together. The bats smothered the crags and slopes of the foothills. Insects in their millions formed a shimmering, molten pond in the main concourse. Men and birds and rangy dogs, all gleaming gold in a sinister phalanx, waited in silence. A sense of dread anticipation carried through the night.

'They're in formation,' the Doctor realised. 'Privates on parade. That's why the golem-bats and their animal mates didn't follow us through the caves, why they only left a skeleton guard for us. They can sense it.'

'Sense what?' Rose asked him.

'Something's coming. Something they stand a chance of beating only if they all work together.' He looked at her, eyes dark and soulful. 'I think war's going to break out tonight.'

'Hey. What the hell is that?' Basel was pointing to a glowing blue light, higher up in the crags, a few hundred metres away. The glow became green as they watched.

The Doctor stared. 'Sub-orbital landing beacon, by the look of it.'

'Thought so,' said Rose, deadpan. 'What does it do?'

'It guides down spaceships.' The Doctor was already setting off towards it. 'That's what the golems are waiting for. Trouble is coming down from the sky. Big trouble.'

'Trouble, Doctor?' Faltato came clattering over the lip of the crag, rubbing his pincers together, his five eyes glinting silver in the moonlight. 'You don't know the meaning of the word.'

'Not him again,' said Basel, shrinking back. Rose took his hand and squeezed it.

'So what are you doing?' the Doctor enquired. 'Bringing down your getaway vehicle, ready to stash the loot?'

'As if you're not after the treasures yourself!' Faltato retorted.

'He's not!' said Rose.

'Why else would you be right here, right now, unless you'd been following our progress from warren to warren?' Faltato sneered. 'Each Valnaxi art warren contains coded directions to find the next – and I have decrypted those pointing the way to the final warren correctly!' He clapped his pincers together. 'All those great works – the *Lona Venus*, *The Flight of the Valwing*, *The Shriek*… Lost for thousands of years – and located by *me*.'

'How many Valnaxi strongholds have you raided?' the Doctor demanded.

'Does it matter?' Faltato said airily.

'They lost the war, their planet, their *spirit*. Their eternal muse, the key to their artistry – shattered by their enemies and turned into a rancid squat.'

'They lost everything,' agreed Faltato. 'Their holdings and acquisitions are forfeit – along with their existence.'

'But you've opened a proper little Pandora's box, haven't you?' The Doctor stabbed a finger down at the gathered golems. 'The Valnaxi defences have been triggered. People have *died*, animals have –'

'Oh, don't be foolish.' The creature's legs brushed and bristled together as he gave a theatrical shrug. 'I hardly designed the defence mechanism, did I? Anyway, there'll be a lot more dead by the time my sponsors are finished here.'

'Sponsors?' The Doctor pulled out the sonic screwdriver and wielded it like a weapon. 'Who's in that spaceship? Who's coming?'

'You'll see.' Faltato slapped out his tongue and lashed the sonic from the Doctor's hand. 'They'll want to meet you, I'm sure.'

'Give that back!'

'They take a dim view of tomb robbers trying to steal their treasures.'

'Theirs?' The Doctor gaped. 'Theirs by what right?'

'By right of conquest!' Faltato snapped, slipping the screwdriver into the pocket of his immaculate suit jacket.

'Oh. My. God.' Rose felt her blood run cold. A dark undulating shape had resolved itself from out of the starry indigo overhead. It was like staring up at the vast, fleshy underbelly of some huge, segmented creature that had come crawling out of the crevices of deepest space. And it was plummeting to earth at an alarming rate. 'What is that?'

'It's a spaceship,' said the Doctor.

'This ain't even happening,' said Basel in a small voice. 'No way.'

Rose wished she could agree. 'Never seen a spaceship like that before.'

'I have.' The Doctor looked at Faltato, pursed his lips. 'So they're your sponsors? Suppose it makes sense. Not happy with wiping out the Valnaxi, they're coming to crush whatever was left behind.'

'Who are?' Rose asked, frowning. But suddenly huge, puckering mouths opened up in the quivering base of the thing. They spat out thick, foul-smelling muck at an incredible rate, and Rose and Basel almost gagged. In a matter of seconds, two entire crop fields were buried beneath a mountain of the stuff. 'The TARDIS,' she breathed. 'Doctor, the TARDIS is under there!'

The strange ship squelched down, using the muck mountain to cushion its impact. A shudder passed through the ranks of the golems. Rose stared transfixed as the sides of the muck-mountain began to shake. Piles of manure were knocked clear and crumbled down the stinking slopes.

Then suddenly the mud was alive with dozens of huge, monstrous shapes, squirming, writhing, forcing their way through. Each was the size of a baby elephant, with a pale, glistening, segmented body like a giant earthworm – Rose couldn't tell where the neck ended and the head began, there were no discernible features. They wore strange suits of crumbling white armour round their wiggling torsos, with special attachments on their stubby arms. As they coiled and slithered down the mudslide, she could see no legs, only the fat, muscular lower body, raw pink segments rippling.

'What are those things?' Basel croaked.

'They're called Wurms,' said the Doctor. 'Fought the Valnaxi across seventeen star systems.'

Rose shook her head. 'Just for that one planet?'

'They'd already taken its neighbours. It was perfectly placed for the Wurms to expand their empire out into space – or for their opponents to land a bridgehead and expand into Wurm territory. They couldn't just leave it alone in case someone else conquered it...' He shrugged. 'It was something like that, anyway. They probably forgot themselves after the first few centuries of war.'

'The Wurms forget nothing,' said Faltato. 'They have crushed the Valnaxi's last efforts to resist and now they will seize the final spoils.'

At the sight of the Wurms, the golems pressed forwards, screeching, roaring and howling towards the enormous mud pile and the writhing invaders.

'So Africa becomes the final battleground,' the Doctor murmured, as the carnage and chaos began.

THIRTEEN

Adiel stared out through the dusty window of the labourers' block, with Fynn and Guwe crouched beside her. She couldn't believe her eyes and ears, and wished she didn't have to believe her nose. It had been her idea to hide and shelter there, thinking they could barricade themselves inside if all else failed. But all else hadn't just failed – it had crashed and burned and gone crazy. Spaceships? Worms as big as a jeep?

Adiel kept pinching herself, desperately hoping she would wake up back in the common room and find Kanjuchi making his usual dreadful coffee.

But she didn't wake up. She only bruised.

The giant worms, caked in white, sticky mud, had a number of guns affixed to a sort of stumpy shoulder. One fired clod after clod of earth from its end with a buzzing, crackling sound. Thick muck splattered over the golems in a sticky wave.

Adiel was close enough to see one of the human golems take a load in the chest. For a few moments, he ignored it and carried on walking. But there were living things in that earth. Squirming, scuttling, *hungry* things. They started devouring the gleaming shield of magma, along with any flesh left beneath.

More gobs of mud fired from the giant earthworms' stubby cannons, seething with hungry life. The man-golem stopped still, his mouth hanging open in a piercing scream as the bugs ate their fill of him. Seconds later there was nothing left but a charred, misshapen skeleton. The same thing was happening again and again, the ranks of gleaming gold giving way to ash and mangled bone as the mud splattered through the golem ranks.

But the flying defenders – the bats, the vultures, the sausage flies – made harder targets and enjoyed more success. They swooped down on the giant worms, greedily tearing chunks from the pink, wrinkled flesh. One of the worms started flailing about in agony, a fluid like wallpaper paste gushing from its gashes. Another sprayed jets of dark liquid from its blind, glistening head: venom maybe, or perhaps it was simply spitting in contempt.

'This can't be real,' breathed Guwe as the noise of the conflict grew louder and louder. He turned and grabbed hold of Fynn by the throat. 'I don't know what stunt you're trying to pull here, Director, or how you managed to… to *drug* me or hypnotise me or whatever you've done –'

'You think you're hallucinating all this?' Fynn knocked his arm away. 'Then go outside, don't let me stop you.'

'Shut up!' Guwe shoved Fynn back against the wall, punched him in the guts, karate chopped him on the back of the neck.

'Stop it!' Adiel shouted.

'I'll teach you to mess with my head,' Guwe hissed, raising his gun, 'by blowing off yours.'

Rose felt her insides churn as the battle got messier, more violent, more and more desperate.

The Doctor surveyed the scene sadly. 'So much for worms being the farmer's friend. I know that they're supposed to turn the soil, but this is taking things a bit too far.'

'It's ruined,' breathed Basel. 'The whole agri-unit. Messed up for ever.'

'What's with the mud-guns?' said Rose.

'An established Wurm method of controlling the guardians' converted servants,' Faltato explained. 'The mud is teeming with insects specially reared to feed on the magma and whatever flesh it is controlling.'

'You've seen battles like this before, then?'

'He's started them,' said the Doctor coldly.

'*My* job is simply to identify that the warren is genuine and not a booby-trapped decoy, as so many are,' Faltato retorted. 'The Valnaxi laid many false trails. Rumour has it that centuries into the conflict, once their race finally accepted they stood no chance of winning, the Valnaxi Council built one final stronghold to house the last and greatest of their race's treasures. This is the place.'

'Oh, so *that's* what you are,' the Doctor murmured, his

eyes wide and dark. 'Not a thief. An expert. An *antiques* expert. The David Dickinson of interstellar art.'

Faltato clacked his pincers. 'I, sir, am a member of the Hadropilatic Fellowship, and an authority on –'

'– hard times, I would guess, since you've hired yourself out to a race as pathologically unstable as the Wurms,' the Doctor went on, casually, but Rose could see the anger creeping into his bland, boyish expression. 'What's your cut, then? What bunce do you get that makes slaughter like this – *devastation* like this – acceptable to you, Faltato?' He bellowed with rage: '*What?*'

'One per cent of the value of the haul, and the credit for identifying the final Valnaxi art warren,' said the creature calmly. 'Once news of *that* gets around, my reputation will be re-established and the phone won't stop ringing.'

Rose stared out dismally over the fighting, then turned to the Doctor. 'Are we just gonna stand around up here and let that happen?'

'No,' said Faltato, 'you are coming with me. The beacon's function is fulfilled. Our means of deliverance is already approaching.'

'What's that?' said Basel distantly. 'Looks like a bubble. Big white bubble.'

'Sort of cocoon, I think, actually,' said the Doctor. 'Or is it an egg sac? Yeah, an air-thrust egg sac! Adaptive technology – Wurms are all for adaptive technology, I read that somewhere. Well, that's lovely, that'll hold us good and strong.' The Doctor looked at Rose. 'I think we'll be off.'

'Stay here,' Faltato snapped. His tongue lashed out, slapping itself around the Doctor's neck with a horrible slurping sound.

'You were right, Rose,' the Doctor gasped. 'Very gifted in the tongue department.'

'Get off him!' Rose shouted.

Basel cried out as another tongue, string-thin, flicked out like a fishing line to hook him round the waist.

'My flossing tongue,' Faltato explained, baring a set of unexpectedly sharp and dazzling teeth as a third tongue splashed out like a long grey eel. 'And *this* is the tongue I eat with…'

It came within a centimetre of touching her arm – but the Doctor dived to the ground, yanking on the tongue so hard it spoiled Faltato's aim. The monster hissed and tightened its slobbering grip on his neck.

'Run – for – it – Rose!' the Doctor panted.

'What about you?' she shouted. But Faltato's tongue was already snaking towards her and while she was free, at least there was a chance that she could do something. Something apart from slipping and falling to her death down the steep foothills, she reflected, and staggered and stumbled down as fast as she could. Her bad ankle burned, like a warning to slow down. Yesterday when she'd done this there had been only a glowing blob to outrun, and for a moment she actually felt nostalgic at the thought.

Because now she was heading down into a war zone. And the fighting was coming her way.

* * *

Adiel watched Guwe standing over Fynn's body, frightened, fuming, one finger curled round the trigger of his gun. 'You can't trick me,' he snarled, gold teeth glinting in his grimace.

'He's unconscious, can't you see that?' she told him. 'What good will killing him do?'

Guwe turned on her, a murderous look in his dark eyes. 'Maybe *you* can explain for him.'

She felt tears rising. 'I can't explain a damn thing.'

He advanced on her, started to smile. Then the smile froze. He jerked up the gun so it pointed at her head.

Before Adiel could react, there was a loud slamming sound behind her, the sound of cracking glass. She whirled round, saw a bat-creature twitching, pressed up against the fractured pane. As she watched, tiny red and white millipedes squirmed over it, reducing it to a tiny, smoking corpse in just a matter of seconds. Adiel pressed her knuckles against her mouth as the skull stayed lodged gruesomely in the centre of the radial cracks while the rest of the body fell away.

Guwe stared through the window, clutching hold of the gun as if he was afraid it might fly away, shaking his head in disbelief. Then, silently, he stormed over to the door.

'Go out there and you're dead,' Adiel warned him.

'I'm not dying here so he can run his sick experiments on *my* corpse,' Guwe snarled.

She stared. 'What did you say?'

'I'll find a way out. I always do.' He slammed the door shut behind him.

Trembling, Adiel stared down at Fynn. He looked like he was sleeping, looked peaceful and innocent.

Experiments. Corpse. Regards from Isako.

She got to her feet, threw open the door. 'I said, what did you say!' Blood roaring through her temples, she chased after him. 'Wait!' she shouted, throwing open the door to the prefab building. But she could barely hear herself over the crackle of the worms' cannons, the screeching of the bats and birds, the yells and whines of dying golems. 'What experiments? Answer me!'

Guwe spared her the briefest of glances back. 'Let me put you out of your misery,' he said casually, raising his gun to shoot her.

'Look out!' screamed a voice from the darkness, as if Adiel hadn't noticed the danger. The same second she ducked down behind the door, she heard a loud, sizzling crackle. Then something kicked the door open, knocked her flying backwards and dived for cover beside her.

It was Rose Tyler.

Adiel's jaw dropped. 'You…'

'Me,' she agreed, a hard look in her eyes. 'Sorry about your friend out there.'

'He wasn't my friend.'

'I'm still sorry.'

Adiel scrambled up, looked out through the dusty glass. Guwe's jaw had dropped too – but there was no skin left to catch it. Millipedes squirmed over the bare skull and there were gaps in its grin where the gold teeth had once been. She looked away, revolted, willing herself not to be sick.

'There was this mud-gun thing,' Rose began awkwardly.

Adiel nodded and pointed to where a couple of the red and white millipedes were wriggling under the door. 'We'd better get out of here,' she croaked, heading back towards the shabby dorm building, her mind turning in ten different dazed directions but feeling weirdly calm. An old boyfriend back in Moundou, one who'd seen action – he'd told her that the more terrifying the situation, the less frightened you felt. There was just no time to be afraid. Now she was starting to understand what he'd meant.

'I thought you and Basel would still be safely out the way of all this in the lava tubes,' she told Rose.

'"Safely" didn't come into it much,' Rose replied coldly. 'Solomon's dead, the Doctor and Basel are being held by some alien thing with too many of everything who's gonna take them to see these giant Wurms, who are blasting the hell out of the golems with killer mud so they can pinch their art treasures.' She stopped for a breath. 'We've got to find a way of getting them out and –'

But Adiel had burst into tears, eyes screwed up tight, fists clenched, trembling.

'Hey.' Rose put her arms round the girl. 'Look, it's all right –'

'I think Director Fynn has been using dead human bodies as part of his research here,' Adiel sobbed. 'My mum and dad among them.'

'Oh…' Rose stared at her, flummoxed. 'OK. Maybe it's not all right.'

Adiel stared at her through her tears, the sounds of the nightmare battle outside growing louder, harsher. 'This could be my last night on Earth,' she said, sniffing loudly. 'So I need to find out fast. Don't I?'

Slowly, Rose nodded and reached out for Adiel's hand. 'Um, yeah. Yeah, s'pose you do.'

'I'm sorry, Adiel.' Fynn's voice made her spin round. 'Life doesn't always come with neat edges.'

He was looking down at the floor, shamefaced and fearful. Flanking him were two of the giant earthworm monsters, rearing up like inflated king cobras. Their tapering, segmented heads peered round blindly beneath their silver helmets, and now she discovered how badly they stank inside their muddy armour. And at this range, Adiel could see that their stubby arms were encased in electronics, enhanced by robotic parts. Their cannons were somehow grafted on to the pale flesh; the combat helmet was almost a part of them.

'Techno-worms,' Rose cringed. 'T'riffic.'

One of the creatures reared up over them and Adiel recoiled in horror. 'You are prisoners of war,' it said in a strained monotone, shuffling forwards on its tail, or its belly, or whatever it was. 'Ambulate ahead of us. Now.'

Rose shrugged helplessly at Adiel. 'At least they're not shooting on sight.'

'Attempt to escape and you will be eaten alive,' the other Wurm informed them, wiggling its cannon.

Numb with fear, Adiel kept her eyes on Fynn, made him her focus as she and Rose were herded ahead of the slithering Wurms and back out into the stifling heat of the noisy night. *Don't let me die*, she prayed to the God she wished she still believed in, *not yet. Not till I know for sure.*

Basel peeped out at the crazy world below through his fingers, as the crusty bubble floated high over the battlefield. This had to be the longest, nastiest night of his life. His senses were spinning from all that he'd seen and done; it was impossible to take in, like stumbling through some hideous nightmare.

The Doctor just sat there, grinning beside Faltato. 'I've never flown by egg sac before,' he confessed cheerily, peering out through the opaque sides. 'How does it work, then?'

'I don't know,' yawned Faltato.

'I reckon it's powered by breaking down bacteria in the lining to create a propulsion jet of gas,' the Doctor went on. 'What do you reckon, Basel?'

'Solomon is dead.' Basel glared at him, massaging his bruised waist from where Faltato had tongue-lashed him. 'He had two kids, and they're gonna want to know what happened and I'm gonna have to tell them... what?' The Doctor said nothing, gazing out over the chaos down below. 'You don't even care, do you?'

'I care about a lot of things,' the Doctor informed him. 'And I've got a lot of questions I want answered. Like, who's in charge round here, Faltato?'

'King Ottak presides over this clew of Wurms,' said Faltato, 'with the assistance of his Knight-Major, Korr.'

The bubble suddenly changed course, dropped sharply from the sky. Basel's heart sank in sympathy. He realised that they were now directly over the Wurm ship. The ship's hull was gently pulsating, almost as if it was breathing.

Somehow the bubble seemed to pass straight through the hull and sank down into a transparent tube. Then suddenly the skin shrank back, like a gum-bubble punctured. The tube melted away and Faltato shoved the Doctor and Basel forwards with his mean little pincers.

They were standing in a messy wreck of a control room. The floor was packed with earth; it felt warm through his shoes, gently quivering. Banks of soil were heaped here and there around controls, which looked like vast, bristling tree roots. Maggoty things squirmed in the piles, wrapping themselves round levers and switches. In place of the sort of sci-fi scanners and monitors Basel had expected, cobwebbed sacs wobbled on mounds of mud here and there; some showed ghostly black-and-white images of the carnage outside, others showed nothing but interference patterns.

Basel gulped. 'This thing was really built by aliens?'

'Nah. Adapted from living organisms. A technological powerhouse built using nature's bounty...' The Doctor paused. 'I've always been able to take or leave Bounties. Prefer Double Deckers. D'you have Double Deckers in Africa, Basel?'

'Prisoners will be silent,' announced a thin, muffled voice from ground level. Basel jumped and swore, while the Doctor stared, fascinated, as two of the huge, white Wurms pushed up from out of the ground in front of them, coiling and flexing like enormous tubes of flesh.

Clumps of wet, white earth clung to their segmented bodies like uniform or armour and were crawling with insect life. The bigger of the two creatures sported a tangle of thick green creepers on top of his glistening, featureless head, like a crown.

'Flex your ambulatory limbs and point downwards!' said the smaller of the two Wurms, his voice clearer now he was above ground.

Basel stared at the creatures in disgust. 'Do what?'

'Kneel,' the Doctor translated.

'At once!' roared the Wurm.

'Do as the Knight-Major orders,' said Faltato, and Basel quickly obeyed.

'Cor!' cried the Doctor. 'It's Korr! And judging by the niff, that's Korr as in "rotten to the…"'

'Abase yourselves at the belly of King Ottak!' Korr said gruffly.

The Doctor waved a hand in front of his nose, put on his glasses and studied the creature closely. 'Which bit is the royal belly?'

Korr squirted a dark fluid into the Doctor's face, so hard it knocked his glasses off his nose. The liquid was rank and salty, and it splashed over Basel's face too, stung his eyes. Quickly the Doctor joined Basel on his knees.

'That is better,' said the crowned Wurm, his voice boomy and bassy, as if it was distorting through an overloaded speaker.

'Stick these bipeds in the cages,' growled Korr. 'They are valueless.'

'The spirited one is not of this world, Majesty,' said

Faltato. 'I believe he is a rival art scout, here to make his own assessment of the haul.'

'I'm not,' the Doctor declared, sticking his dripping glasses back in his pocket. 'As it is, I'm just travelling through. But I'd take very good care of me – very, very, *very* good care – and you know why?' He stood back up. 'Because you're going to need me.'

'We need no one and nothing,' boomed King Ottak, writhing in anger like a fat, blind serpent. 'Faltato, have you located the deactivation plaque?'

'I have, Your Majesty,' Faltato replied graciously, five eyelids fluttering. 'It was well hidden, as ever. But alas, deactivation will not be straightforward. It lies buried beneath a rock-fall.'

'You have the coordinates?'

'Naturally I do, sire.'

'Deactivation plaque?' the Doctor wondered. 'Suppose the Valnaxi would want to get back in some day and pick up their valuables – if they'd won, of course.'

'Do not speak such blasphemy in my presence!' King Ottak roared, squirming over with alarming speed, like a snake on steroids. 'The Valnaxi could never win. We are the conquerors of space, the destroyers of worlds. And Earth will soon rank among them.'

The Doctor looked up at him coolly. 'Oh?'

'We shall wipe out the Valnaxi guardians, seize their artworks, lay waste to their shrines and devastate this entire planet. Every last stinking spore of the Valnaxi must be wiped from the biosphere.'

'And why d'you wanna do that, then?'

'To avenge our dead.'

'Oh. Right.' The Doctor pulled a face. 'Just a thought – d'you think the dead will take much notice?'

Korr reared up and lashed out at the Doctor with his tapering head, sending him sprawling into one of the control mounds in a shower of mud. 'Insolent biped,' he wheezed.

'Call me all the names you like.' The Doctor glared up at him. 'I won't let you do this.'

'Ten-toed scum, you cannot stop us! We shall wring from your world what nutrients we can, then leave it barren and dead, a final monument to the art of destruction.'

Basel looked at the Doctor. 'He's mad,' he whispered.

King Ottak shivered with what might have been rage or laughter, agitating the insects in his stinking soil.

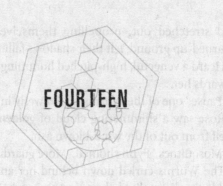

FOURTEEN

A new day was poking out its nose from night's blanket. Rose wished the light away, wished the dawn light would darken till she could see nothing at all.

She felt like she was being marched through hell.

Once outside the main complex, the stench, the heat and the sights and sounds of battle fixed every step with horror. Corpses, chewed up and charred, lay scattered all about, yet still the golems kept coming – bats and birds, even gleaming, mutated Wurms – and still the dull wet splats of the mud guns echoed on. For a few moments she had been grateful for the stinking smoke drifting across the concourse that hid the worst from view – until she realised it was ash from roasted bones, and she was breathing it in.

Adiel's hand found her own and Rose gripped hold of it. Fynn was walking ahead of them, leading the way as if he needed to act the big Director even now. The Wurms were lumbering along behind them. Rose could hear the sickening squelching of their bodies as they bunched up and stretched out, propelling themselves along the churned-up ground, felt their shadows falling over her.

Heard a vengeful, high-pitched humming noise sweep towards her.

'Pause,' one of the Wurms hissed wetly in her ear.

Rose saw a shimmering cloud of golden smoke pull itself from out of the wind-blown ash.

'Mosquitoes,' Fynn shouted. 'More guardians!'

The Wurms curled down behind her and Adiel, and suddenly she realised they weren't just being marched ahead of their captors. They were human shields. Rose stood dead still, but before she could even start to think of what to do, the cloud of mosquitoes parted like a gauzy curtain around them and moved on.

Adiel was almost breaking Rose's hand she was squeezing so tight. 'How come they didn't attack us?'

Next second, Rose felt sticky wet flesh slapped up against her cheek as one of the Wurms pressed against her. The words seeped into her ear, accusingly. 'You ally yourselves with the Valnaxi creatures?'

'Look out!' Adiel shouted, as a livid gold blur beat a path through the smog, an eagle or something, snapping at the Wurms. Fluid jetted over Rose's shoulder as her guard's flesh was torn by beak or claw. The Wurm holding her gave a gurgling roar of anger and coiled itself about her, soggy segments contracting against her skin as it writhed upwards, lifted her kicking and screaming into the path of the golem. *It'll rip me to pieces*, she thought.

But the misshapen eagle gave a screech of anger and backed off.

The other Wurm grabbed Adiel in much the same way, held her up like she was a living crucifix seeing off a swooping vampire. The eagle-thing soon gave up and went away.

Rose caught Adiel's eye; they connected in baffled expressions: *I dunno what happened either.*

'Continue your ambulation,' Adiel's Wurm told Fynn.

'Gonna put me down?' Rose said as casually as she could.

'No,' the Wurm replied, a deep gouge in its face the only visible feature as it turned to its comrade. 'Hurry. We must report to the king. The guardians do not attack the human bipeds.'

'Since when?' said Adiel, gasping as the Wurms set off again. 'What's changed?'

Basel wiped sweat from his face, longing for a line of passive pills and a cold drink of water to wash them down with. He watched King Ottak squirming about the control room, peering at each of the crackling muddy monitor screens in turn, conferring with Korr. They were getting reports from the field, Basel supposed – at least it was taking the heat off him and the Doctor, sat deep in thought beside him.

Then suddenly Korr steamed over, raining dollops of smelly white soil down all around, and the heat was turned back up to baking.

'Explain the nature of your people's alliance with the Valnaxi.'

'We haven't got one!' Basel protested.

'But I can see why you might think so,' said the Doctor, getting slowly back up to his feet, staring past Basel at one of the monitors.

It showed an aerial view of Adiel and Rose in the grip of two Wurms, Fynn in front of them, being herded across the ruined concourse.

'They've caught everyone,' Basel breathed. Then he realised that gathered all around were golems. Insects, birds, dogs – a writhing mutated Wurm too – moving along like a grisly escort, matching them pace for pace. 'What's that lot doing? Waiting for the moment to strike?'

'Or to step in and try to save them,' the Doctor murmured. He raised his voice, turning to the king. 'I hope you treat your prisoners well.'

'Afraid for yourself, Doctor?' Faltato sneered.

'Afraid for all of you,' he said simply, no trace of humour in his voice now, 'because if anything bad happens to Rose and I think it's your fault…'

'I have never observed such behaviour in the guardian drones,' said Korr, ignoring him. 'None have acted this way in any of the other warrens.'

'It is as if they have been programmed not to attack human bipeds,' mused the king. 'And yet we have seen converted humans in the ranks of our enemies.'

'No doubt the deactivation plaque was damaged in the rock-fall,' said Faltato. 'It is malfunctioning.'

Ottak nodded. 'Perhaps.'

'It's interesting.' The Doctor was smiling. 'Don't you think that's interesting, Basel? I told King Ottak he'd need me. Didn't I tell him!'

Ottak shuffled slowly towards them, his voice quiet and dangerous. 'What assistance can you offer us?'

'Well, for a start…' The Doctor pointed to a static-filled screen, unfazed. 'The Valnaxi know your bio-tech, right? They can detect your scan frequencies and block them – so you can't see inside that mountain.' He held up the data-get. 'I can.'

'Irrelevant,' Korr said, though still he stretched out his segmented body towards them, straining obscenely to see. 'We have Faltato's intelligence on the warren.'

'*Limited* intelligence.' The Doctor winked at Faltato. 'He can give you coordinates for the deactivation panel. Well, whoop-de-doo!' He patted the data-get. '*This* baby can show you the entire layout of the Valnaxi warren at a glance, allow you to pinpoint every guardian in the place. You can have a butcher's at their defences, plan how to strike at the heart of their stronghold.'

'Don't trust him, Knight-Major,' Faltato twittered.

'Oh, shut your slit,' the Doctor taunted him. 'Got you going, haven't I? Eh? Touched a nerve or what! Just 'cause *you* didn't think to make one.'

A mechanical probe-arm whirred out from a stump of raw flesh growing from Korr's torso and took hold of the data-get. He presented it to his king.

'Think they'll buy it?' Basel asked.

The Doctor nodded. 'Think they'll try and *take* it.'

'Then what?'

'Wait and see. In about, oooh, three, two, one…'

Korr turned and waved his blind, quivering head at the

Doctor. 'Your scanning machine cannot function as you say it can.'

He winked at Basel, placed one hand behind his back. 'Let me guess – you've noticed the data-get's memory's getting clogged by the amount of scan data available, right?' Basel saw him discreetly drop some tiny circuits and press them into the dirt beneath his heel. 'Memory wafers! They'll fix it up in three seconds flat…'

'Where can memory wafers be acquired?' Korr wheezed.

The Doctor looked at Basel, wide-eyed and innocent. 'Oooh, I dunno. Lab in the unit's probably our best bet, wouldn't you say, Basel? Specially as there'll be other bipeds loitering there. Ones the Wurms haven't caught yet.'

Basel frowned. 'What ones?'

'The staff.' The Doctor gave him a *play-along* look. 'The unit offers the only shelter. Most likely place they'll go.' He strolled over to a monitor which now showed Adiel, Fynn and Rose being hustled into some kind of muddy prison area. He tapped the image of Fynn before it vanished inside something that looked like a giant walnut. 'That man is the Director of this complex.'

'He is a prisoner of war,' stated Korr. 'Like all prisoners, he will be questioned for information on the enemy, then executed and allowed to enrich the soil with the gush of his bodily fluids.'

'One approach,' the Doctor conceded. 'But think about it. Aren't *all* your prisoners worth more to you alive? These humans seem to be the most powerful defence you've got right now. And Director Fynn's staff in the unit will surrender to him if he orders them to – no question! They'll give you no trouble, and you'll get yourselves a job lot of living shields.'

'Patrol seven found no further trace of biped activity in the unit grounds,' Korr argued.

King Ottak seemed to consider. 'But battle analysis supports the theory that the guardian drones are not attacking bipeds...'

Basel looked at the Doctor and spoke in the softest of voices. 'What happens if they ask Fynn and find out you're lying?'

'Then they'll kill me a little sooner,' said the Doctor simply.

Rose had never been happier to be locked away. Her ribs were bruised, her clothes slimy and damp, and while she didn't feel exactly safe, at least the ordeal of crossing the battleground was over. They'd reached the Wurm ship and entered down a steep, winding tunnel of wet earth, eerily lit by luminous green bugs scuttling in the filth, all the way to some kind of holding area. The cell was dimly lit, hard and knobbly like walnut shell, and only a little bigger. But at least it was just her, Fynn and Adiel – no Wurms or golems.

Not that Adiel and Fynn seemed ecstatic at being in such close proximity. They sat in a silence as uncomfortable as the bony cell floor, with Rose squashed up in the middle. She had a feeling that she was about to become a referee.

'Just tell me it's true, Fynn,' Adiel said slowly. 'Then tell me why.'

Fynn didn't answer.

Rose placed a hand on Adiel's. 'What happened to your parents?'

'There had been fighting in Moundou. Didn't think much about it at first – I mean, there's always been fighting, probably always will be.' Adiel shrugged. 'My parents were driving across the Chad border to help at one of the refugee camps. There was an ambush, witnesses said they were shot.'

'Why?' whispered Rose. 'Why do that?'

'Different factions, different ethnic groups vying for power and money and good land... So rebels fight the government, rebels fight among themselves, they stage shows of strength and take territory...'

'Sounds familiar,' said Rose sadly, wondering how long the Wurm war had gone on.

'In the end, they're not just fighting the government, they're attacking the civilians they were supposed to protect. But this little campaign was different.' Adiel looked at Fynn, whose head was still hanging down. 'The rebels didn't just kill and loot from the innocent. They kidnapped people. Beat them, bundled them into their trucks and drove off with them.'

Fynn sat up a little straighter. 'I lost my father to scum like that. Sacrificed for a ragbag cause. For nothing at all.'

'Then why did you deal with filth like Roba Isako?' hissed Adiel. 'What did Guwe mean when he talked about your experiments –'

'How many people have died in this conflict?' Fynn shouted at her. 'Centuries of ethnic violence, of factions set on wiping each other out, on gaining power for themselves. The bloodshed goes on, how can it ever be resolved? And with the death and disruption comes disease, comes poverty, comes famine. *More* death.' His whole body was shaking. 'Death with no meaning on such a scale. But if the deaths must go on, I can *give* them meaning. No one should die in vain.'

Rose suddenly felt more scared than ever. 'What're you on about?'

'There is not enough food to go round, not enough land on which to grow it,' said Fynn, suddenly calm and controlled again. 'But imagine if I could farm the dead…'

A thick silence settled inside the shell.

'You bought bodies from Isako,' Adiel croaked.

'I had to,' said Fynn quietly. 'I needed preliminary results if I was to get proper funding!'

'You took dead bodies here and you tried to grow your *fungus* on them?'

'It was too soon,' he said bitterly. 'My work was not yet advanced enough. Only by making the fungus toxic and useless as a food source could I –'

'You're sick.' Rose remembered the cave of skeletons, the cobwebby fur on their bones. 'I've seen the evidence, Adiel. There's bones, just… just lying there.' She rounded on him. 'No wonder you wanted that side of the tunnels shut off, so no one would ever find out. What you did was disgusting. The dead deserve respect.'

'We owe respect to the living!' Fynn argued just as

hotly. 'Would you rather these people died in vain? For nothing, like *my* father? Don't you think they would rather know they helped others to live?'

'You had no right!' Adiel shouted. 'What about my parents? Were they among the dead you used?'

'I never knew the subjects' identities,' Fynn protested. 'Isako had already taken their belongings, ID, everything.'

Adiel stared, incredulous. 'Then... then for all this, I'll never know.'

'I wasn't proud of what I did, but I had no choice,' he went on. 'The soul flees the body after death – I performed my experiments on the empty shell, discarded.'

'It's horrible,' said Rose simply.

'Don't you see?' Fynn stared imploringly at her. 'Only radical thinking can break the cycle of poverty, famine disease and death and bring new hope, new life –'

'And a new form of bio-piracy,' came a familiar voice from just outside.

'Doctor!' With a surge of hope, Rose leaned over Adiel and pressed her hands up against the side of the prison. 'Doctor? Get us out of here!'

'Um, slight problem there –'

'Shut it!' came a loud, rattling snarl.

Rose jumped even as her heart sank, as with a creaking, sucking noise a hatch sprang open in front of her. 'All bipeds are to leave the cells!' rasped the Wurm waiting just outside. It wasn't wearing a helmet like the other one, but had more electronic gadgets around its broad, soily neck. The Doctor and Basel stood helpless in the grip of freaky Faltato just behind. Rose looked at Adiel to see how she'd react to this latest arrival – but she didn't. Perhaps she'd seen so much horror that another monster meant nothing to her. Or perhaps after finding a monster like Fynn, others just couldn't measure up.

'Rose!' The Doctor peered in at her and the others with a worried expression. 'You all right?'

'About as un-all right as it's possible to be,' said Rose.

Korr moved forwards to face Fynn. 'You are the leader of these bipeds?'

Rose jumped in. 'No one's gonna listen to a word he says –'

'– unless you let him speak to them in person,' said the Doctor quickly.

'Very well. Prisoners Doctor and Leader, you will accompany me to the complex. If you try to escape, you will be killed, ingested and excreted in casts.' He nodded his fat, tapering head. 'For extra protection, I shall also take the pale creature.'

'Mum's fake tan was a big success, then,' said Rose sourly as she was directed to join the Doctor and Fynn.

'Why not let everyone come with us?' the Doctor suggested brightly. 'Extra protection for you.'

Korr shook his big, blank, belligerent head. 'If bipeds may ambulate without fear of attack, we can use them to start emptying the warren of its art treasures.'

'Since you've already cracked open the treasure chambers *without* first deactivating the plaque, Doctor,' Faltato said, 'the least we can do is take advantage of your generosity and help ourselves.'

'We shall proceed,' Korr stated. 'Once bipeds in hiding have been located, they will join with these two to form a workforce and start transporting the treasures to the ship.'

'*I* shall be supervising,' said Faltato primly. 'I am needed in person to ensure that no pieces are overlooked or mishandled during the clearance.'

'And to ensure that no Wurms die because *you're* taking the risks for them,' said the Doctor brightly. 'Isn't that thoughtful of you? That's so thoughtful!'

'Wurms are the biggest threat to the Valnaxi defences, which makes them the prime targets,' Faltato assured him. 'But should it prove necessary, believe you me, Doctor, your friends will form an effective shield for me too.'

'Don't bet on it,' muttered Basel.

'We leave at once,' rasped Korr. 'King Ottak wishes the campaign concluded with all speed.'

'So do I,' said the Doctor grimly. 'Let's go.'

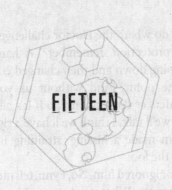

FIFTEEN

Back out on the stinking, ash-shrouded battleground, Rose, the Doctor and Fynn were having to hold hands around the Wurm soldier. It was as if they were playing ring-a-ring-o'-roses, surrounding and shielding it, trying to match its obscene, wriggling movements as it squelched through the mud and bones.

Fynn was keeping quiet, but his fingers were clutching at Rose's. She didn't look at him. Whatever the Doctor might say, the stuff Fynn had done was wrong and she couldn't find it in herself to feel any understanding. He could have done things differently – but he knew how people would have reacted, so he'd gone his own way. Now she couldn't help but wonder if he'd used bits of the bodies or everything in one go, how long each one had lasted, how he'd stored them away in his caves, out of sight and the sun, his grisly little secret –

'Lovely stroll,' said the Doctor brightly. 'How about a bit of conversation?'

'Shut it,' said Korr.

'Or you'll do what?' the Doctor challenged. 'Out here, we're your protection, remember?' A handful of bats came swooping down and then changed course, as if to reinforce the point. 'And without us you won't get memory wafers *or* slave labour. So if it's all the same to you, I think we'll talk. I think we'll have a right old gas.'

The Wurm made a hissing, straining noise, like an elephant on the loo.

The Doctor ignored him. 'So, Fynn, tell me more about your experiments. What went wrong? I remember you saying that fungus could grow on just about anything – it *feeds* on the decay of organic matter, doesn't it?'

Rose glared at him. 'Adiel's parents might have been used for mushroom compost and you want to *chat* about it?'

'Could be important. Go on, Fynn.'

'The genetic structures of human and fungus are incompatible,' Fynn said quietly, trying not to slip in a patch of wet mud. 'Animal cells have semi-porous membranes controlling what passes in and out, maintaining function and integrity of the cellular processes. Fungi have cell *walls*, protecting the insides from physical movement which could prove harmful.'

'Of course,' said the Doctor. 'That's got to be it. Could be our only chance.'

Rose stared. 'So you're glad he did experiments on dead people, then?'

The Doctor shrugged. 'The road to hell is paved with good intentions.'

'I've seen enough of hell lately, thanks –' Rose broke off

as weird birds squawked and flapped somewhere overhead; scouting out the battlefield maybe, or trying to find a way of reaching the Wurms.

'Tell me, Korr,' said the Doctor. 'Have you seen any of the magma-form guardians out on the front line?'

'They cower in fear of us,' the Wurm hissed. 'As do all our enemies.'

'Yeah, yeah. Funny, though, isn't it? Hanging back and picking on the likes of Solomon when they're actually the best fighters.'

'Maybe the guardians wanted to get back at Solomon for bringing the roof down on their golden plaque thing,' Rose suggested.

The Doctor frowned. 'You what?'

'Adiel saw him do it. He must have found it a while back and decided to bury it.'

'Golden plaque, eh? That must be the deactivation panel Faltato mentioned...' He frowned. 'I'd like to take a look at that myself.'

'Perhaps you will,' said Korr, 'when you join your fellows in slavery, clearing the caverns.'

'I think I mentioned,' said the Doctor sharply, 'you should treat us with a bit more respect. While we're here, nothing's gonna attack –'

'Look out!' Rose screamed as a glowing ball of fiery energy came rolling out of the ashen mist.

It was one of the guardians, tired of the tunnels perhaps. Ready to rumble.

Making straight for her.

She pulled her hands away and staggered back,

breaking the circle. The Wurm spat dark juices at the creature, which crackled and hissed over its gleaming skin. But it ignored him, grew larger, surged out and slopped against her feet.

Rose shouted out, though it didn't actually hurt – not for the first couple of seconds anyway. The Doctor grabbed hold of her hand to try and pull her clear, but she could already feel a searing heat rising up through her legs, blistering her from the inside. For a moment her eyes met the Doctor's – wide, horrified and helpless – then she screwed them up as the pain tore through her, as the guardian flowed up her body, drawing her into the furnace of its form.

Her vision burned blood red for a moment, as weird shadows started to solidify in her sight. Then she was dissolved and gone and knew nothing.

Fynn stared in terror, shock rooting him to the spot as the magma form flowed over the flailing form of the Doctor's friend. One moment she was struggling, the next she was frozen, limbs splayed out, a golden statue. But she didn't remain still like the others and she didn't attack. She turned and ran away.

The guardian retreated after her like an obedient dog as the Wurm fired its stubby cannon. Mud and insects splattered over the ground just beside it, but the guardian kept moving, soon swallowed by the ghostly swirl of sand and ashes just as Rose was. The Wurm fired after them wildly, blast after blast.

Then something grabbed Fynn by both shoulders,

spun him around. He started to shout out, but a bony hand clamped down on his mouth.

It was the Doctor, face pressed up close, eyes dark and wild. Fynn could see the pain there, the anger, the refusal to face up to a truth so hard. It was like seeing into his own eyes, the day he'd found out about his father.

The Doctor threw him towards the nearby complex. 'Run!'

Fear took over where momentum left off and Fynn started to work his legs harder, faster. Even so, the Doctor overtook him effortlessly.

'Stop!' the Wurm roared after them. 'Bipeds will cease ambulation!'

'Not right now they won't,' the Doctor called back.

Fynn heard the squelch of the cannon, flinched as a huge clod of mud splattered against the wall of the complex, brushed frantically at his clothes in case one of the insect things had landed there. Saw the Doctor holding open the door to the lab unit and threw himself inside, shivering so hard he could barely draw breath.

'Get up,' the Doctor snapped, slamming the door shut behind them and locking it.

'Don't understand...' Fynn rolled over on to his back. 'What made the magma form attack us now?'

'It didn't attack *us*, it attacked Rose.' The Doctor hauled him back up by the shoulders, pale and trembling. 'First, Solomon – then Rose.'

'Who next?' Fynn whispered.

'I need you alert,' the Doctor snapped. 'Be alert. Your planet needs lerts.'

Fynn stared at him blankly. 'That Wurm will be after us.'

'Of course he will. So we've got to work fast.' He reached in his pocket, then scowled. 'And without the sonic screwdriver. Come on… the lab. We'll have to lock ourselves in.'

'What are you planning?'

'Those lovely experiments of yours,' the Doctor said. 'I'm guessing you tried to create an interface between human flesh and fungus at a cellular level, right?'

Fynn nodded, tried to focus his thoughts. 'I tried to create hybrid cells. I had some limited success, but –'

'Well, luckily I'm *not* limited, not by anything.' The Doctor bundled him away down the deserted corridor. 'I'm a genius. So I'm gonna succeed where you failed, right?' He closed a set of fire doors and bolted them shut. 'And I'm gonna do it in about five minutes flat. Easy.' He set off again, practically carrying Fynn by the scruff of his neck. 'Easy-peasy.'

Fynn pulled free of the Doctor's grip, tried to hold still a moment. 'But why, what are you –'

The Doctor dragged him along by the arm instead. 'The guardian converted the fungus into a sentry entity, but your 'shrooms threw off their chains – *alien protein* chains – and re-established their original form.' He strode along to the lab and kicked open the door. 'That's got to be down to the basic cellular mismatch. If we can come up with a way to harden the cell membranes into cell walls just long enough to drive out the magma infection –'

'– without killing the subject –'

'– then, hey presto! We'll have an anti-golem serum. And that could be Rose's one chance. If we can only reach her…' He slammed his hand down on the bench. 'We *will* reach her. Fungus samples! Where where where?'

Fynn hurried to the hidden safe in the wall, keyed in the access code. 'I return to the theoretical work whenever I can, but still I'm no nearer a breakthrough.'

'That's why you had to shift towards guano and growth chambers?'

'When the crop is hardy enough, I can continue with the real work – and with official sanction, proper resources…' He started selecting the likeliest of his aborted preparations. 'Edet Fynn, the man who saved the world. That is my dream. Time will tell.'

'Won't it just.' The Doctor looked at him sadly, as if he knew something Fynn didn't. 'Well, my dream's jumping the queue right now, so let's shift.'

'Doctor, you had this idea in mind *before* your friend was infected, didn't you? Why?'

'There are two sides in any war,' said the Doctor, locking the door and dragging a workbench over to place against it. 'Tried persuading the Wurms to pick a fight somewhere else – didn't work out. But the Valnaxi fought the Wurms for ages and ages. They might just know of some weakness we can use to end this carnage, before the Earth cops it.'

'But they were all wiped out.'

'*Something's* playing god to those golems. A battle

computer or a defence entity. Something that might be able to help us.' Straining, he heaved the lead box with the bat inside it on top of the workbench. 'So, I thought I could whiz up some golem-repellent to use on myself.' He grabbed a data-get, powered up and trained it on the first of the phials Fynn produced from the safe. 'The magma should infect me like it did the fungus, but with any luck it won't be able to take full control. Then I'll be able to commune with the magma forms without becoming one of them.'

'Experimenting on yourself?' Fynn powered up the gene-translator, stared at him. 'You'd take that risk?'

'Things we do to save the world, eh, Fynn?' The Doctor grinned as he rolled up his sleeve, as if he was actually enjoying this in some twisted way. 'Now, we'll use some of my blood as a base. It's as clever as the rest of me – highly adaptive, with regenerative properties. Have to remove the extra-cellular matrix so it's compatible with all other Earth animal life, of course…'

'*Earth* animal life?'

The Doctor pointed to the lead box. 'Then we can test it on Tolstoy the bat in there, see if he can throw off the golem effect. Of course, it won't put right the genetic mutation, but…' He studied the data-get's readout – then slapped it down on a bench. 'Right! We'll start from scratch, I think. Instead of trying to merge a cell wall with a cell membrane, how about we build one around the other? A wall that will decay before permanent damage can occur, leaving the original cell intact.' He nodded to himself. 'We can adapt the Kilbracken technique.'

Fynn frowned. 'The what?'

'Chemical parlour trick. Instead of cloning the cells, you conjure a sort of 3D photocopy.'

Fynn's head was spinning. 'But how can you know if it will stop the magma force from taking you over?'

'I can't for sure. But we can run a quick trial using this.' Suddenly Adiel's necklace was dangling from the Doctor's fingers, the tiny specks of gold glowing in the crystals. 'Hopefully not enough of the substance to be really harmful but enough to test our solution. Now maybe you could shut up, think positive and get working.' He looked up from the data-get, his eyes burning into Fynn's. 'Remember what we saw happen to Kanjuchi, the way he swelled up, mutated? Same as the vulture and poor old Tolstoy here, as all the golems.' He prepared to take his blood sample. 'That's the point where body chemistry is too far gone to reverse the damage caused by the Valnaxi pathogen. Rose will *not* reach that point – OK?'

Fynn nodded grimly and started preparing a laser syringe. 'But how long before that Wurm reaches *us*?'

The battering of locked doors carried from outside.

'Start a stopwatch and we can do a little experiment,' the Doctor suggested, holding out his arm. 'Maybe they'll publish our findings.'

Fynn activated the syringe. 'Posthumously,' he murmured.

Basel huddled close to Adiel as Faltato dragged them through the narrow, red-lit passages. There had been no sign of golems or blobs or rebels or anything else – it was just them and the alien monster from hell, two of its slavering tongues wrapped around their waists.

They had used a weird, bubble-like container to cross from the Wurm ship to the eastern lava tubes, floating high over the battlefield. The golems were fighting with frightening fury to keep the Wurms away from the double doors that gave entrance to the caverns, but had left Adiel, Basel and even Faltato alone. Basel figured that the Wurms were a bigger threat than three random aliens, and Adiel guessed he was right. What other explanation could there be?

Now two more of the crusty, translucent containers bobbed slowly after them, ready to be filled with Valnaxi treasures and sent back to the Wurm ship.

'A brief diversion,' Faltato announced suddenly. 'I want to check on something. There's something fishy going on.'

You could say that, thought Adiel wearily; as understatements went, it was up there with *war is hell*.

He swung them into a narrow tunnel she recognised, one that ended in a huge pile of rocks. Basel could see a golden haze beneath it, like fireflies swarming.

He turned to Adiel. 'This is what you were gonna show me and Rose before you dumped us in the other tunnel?'

'Yeah,' she said. 'The thing I saw Solomon bury.'

'The deactivation plaque,' said Faltato haughtily, withdrawing his tongue. 'Study the rock-fall. Assess what tools you'll need to clear it.'

Basel walked in silence along the tunnel to see.

'So, this deactivation plaque can turn off the golems and the guardians?' said Adiel behind him.

'If fed the right security codes, it will deactivate the warren's defences,' agreed Faltato, before adding heavily, 'Hence the name.'

'Then why isn't it better protected?' she argued. 'The magma should have thanked Solomon, not killed him. Why isn't this place crawling with golems?'

'That Wurm thing said this place wasn't working right,' Basel reminded her. 'But... there were even scorpions and spiders and things in that crummy chamber where Solomon got killed. So why not here?' But even as he approached the rubble-strewn plaque, the rocks began to rumble and stir. One toppled off the pile and skittered down to land at his feet.

Basel frowned, tried to lift it. The thing should have weighed a ton, but this was rough and light like pumice. He pushed at some more of the debris, which either tumbled from the pile or crumbled to dust.

'This ain't right,' he called back. 'The rock's gone funny.'

Faltato galloped towards him, dragging Adiel along behind. 'The rock has been exposed to some kind of intense energy field,' he muttered. 'Just hours ago the rock was solid enough... It is as if the binding force has been extracted.' He shook his pointed head as he swept more of the dusty debris clear, exposing the plaque. Then all five eyes narrowed in what might have been a frown.

'What is it?' Adiel asked warily.

'This isn't a deactivation plaque,' he murmured. 'It's

designed to look like one, but the data-feed is a fake.' He gestured with a pair of pincers to a hole in the plaque, where lights like magma glowed inside, linked by glassy tubes. 'I don't know what this technology does, but it shouldn't be here.'

'Well, if this thing doesn't deactivate anything, what *does* it do?' breathed Adiel.

'What *did* it do?' Faltato corrected her. 'It has been damaged, hence the energy leak. But its purpose...' His legs rattled together, a sinister, unsettling sound. 'Why am I discussing this with bipeds?'

Adiel shrugged. 'Perhaps you should tell the Wurms.'

'The Valnaxi block their signals, they won't be able to hear me.' Faltato looked troubled. 'Later, perhaps.'

He turned and shuffled back up the side tunnel.

'Why *was* he discussing it with us?' Basel murmured.

Adiel regarded the monster bobbing about on his endless legs. 'I think because he's scared,' she said.

SIXTEEN

Fynn pulled the latest sample from the centrifuge, prepared a slide and slotted it under the intron microscope. Maybe *this* one would… 'No. No good,' he reported. 'The fungus cell "photocopies" are forming a barrier round your own cells, but they break down in seconds.'

'That's a bit rubbish…' The Doctor was on the opposite side of the lab, bent over beakers and jars of foul-smelling chemicals. 'Mix in a little of samples A and E.' Suddenly he jerked his head up, hair waving about wildly. 'Oh, hang on, A and E – Accident and Emergency, that doesn't sound hopeful, does it? Tell you what, make it A and H. AH! Ahhhhhh.' He smiled and nodded to himself. 'Yeah, that sounds more like it. Should make the cell walls less reactive so they'll last longer.'

'But even if this works, how are you going to administer the cure?' asked Fynn. 'You remember Kanjuchi… The skin hardens like metal, so no syringe will –'

'It's all right, I've thought of that,' the Doctor told him, holding up a data-get. 'I've adapted this thing. Now it's a data-*give* as well. When the serum's perfected we can scan it – then broadcast it as an electro-chemical irradiation.'

Fynn stared, speechless. 'You subverted the D-G's entire function in just a few minutes?'

The Doctor looked puzzled. 'Course I did. Rose's life is at stake. Now worry about your own work!'

Fynn did as he was told, in a baffled daze. Everything the Doctor instructed him to do seemed to fly in the face of all established genetic theory. And yet it was working – after a fashion. 'How long do you think you can make the cells endure?'

'Dunno,' he said. 'Long enough, I hope.'

There was a crash from not far down the corridor. Fynn shuddered. 'That Wurm will be here to catch us and kill us any minute.'

'On the case,' the Doctor informed him, holding up a couple of stoppered phials. 'Whipped up an explosive mixture in my spare time. Don't stop working – I'll take the other door, cut through the common room and double back round to draw Korr away.' He slapped down one of the phials on Fynn's workbench. 'If the Wurm gets past me, use this. But hide under the bench first – it's a big bang and it'll probably bring the roof down on you.'

Fynn stared at the phial, then turned his attention to mixing the samples. 'Be careful, Doctor.'

'Yeah. One day.' He ran to the far door, threw it open and ran out into the corridor.

The barricade jumped as the Wurm slammed itself against the main doors. 'I can smell you, bipeds,' Korr hissed. 'Return to me or die.'

Fynn stared at the door the Doctor had taken; it was still standing ajar. He could run too. Hide. Wait for all this to be over. With a tremor of fear, he realised that the Doctor could have done exactly that. What if he'd run out, leaving Fynn behind as a distraction, with nothing more to protect him than a phial full of bad smells?

Then he remembered the pain in the man's eyes at what had happened to Rose and went back to work with renewed determination.

'Life from death,' he murmured, mixing his samples together. 'Life from death.'

The Doctor pelted through the darkened corridors, working his way round back to the lab block in a wide circle, ready to confront Korr. He couldn't afford to waste much time on the Wurm; if Rose was to stand the tiniest chance, he had to be ready to move the moment Fynn finished the concoction.

If it didn't work, with the TARDIS buried under tons of alien earth, there was no chance left for any of them.

He reached the lab block, ran on and on until at last he kicked open the final set of double doors and saw the Wurm slinging its fat, tumescent body against the main lab. The barricade looked set to collapse any moment.

'Korr!' the Doctor bellowed.

'So.' The Wurm writhed, stretched out its blind head towards him. 'The little biped with the big mouth.'

'This is your last chance. I'm warning you – leave this place now or you'll *never* leave it.'

'Threats, little biped?' Korr hissed. 'If you had the means and will to destroy me, you would have launched a surprise attack from within the laboratory you have defended. Therefore, this is a distraction tactic. You wish to stop me from entering the laboratory.'

'I don't have time for this!' The Doctor held the phial above his head. 'This *can* destroy you. Don't make me use it.'

Korr raised the stump at his shoulder and, with a hydraulic hiss, a slim metal tube rotated into position. '*This* weapon can destroy your laboratory. I can fire it before your projectile can touch me. Unless you surrender now, I shall do so.'

'Do that and you'll destroy the memory wafers you need to power the visual device I gave to your king,' the Doctor countered. 'We'll both come out losers.'

'You are creating a weapon in this laboratory,' Korr rumbled, 'a powerful weapon that will stop us from using your see-through device.'

'No! It's not a weapon –'

'You think I am stupid?' roared the Wurm.

'Yes! Because which bit don't you understand? *Lower – that – gun!*'

'You were warned, biped.'

With an electric whine, Korr powered up his weapon.

The Doctor took a deep breath and drew back his arm, ready to hurl the phial.

And then the doors of the lab blew open with the force

of a massive explosion – an explosion that had gone off *inside*.

Korr gave a retching, gurgling screech as glass and brick and metal spat out from the heart of the explosion, tearing great chunks from his body. Black smoke belched out a moment later, hiding the gore from view.

'Fynn!' the Doctor shouted. He shoved the phial in his pocket, picking his way through the debris and the thick, oily smog into the ruined laboratory.

Most of the ceiling had fallen in and the only light was from a single flickering fluorescent. He looked about frantically – then discerned Director Fynn's head and upper body protruding from beneath a broken bench half-buried under rubble.

'Doctor?' Fynn said very calmly. 'Would you come here?'

A moment later the Doctor was crouched beside him. 'You threw the phial.' He saw the blood trickling from the man's mouth, saw his eyes slowly glazing. 'That was brave of you.'

'If that thing had fired, the serum…' Fynn murmured. 'For death to have meaning, life must have it too.' He pointed feebly to something. The lead box was open and on its side. A twisted, misshapen figure lay within, frosted with concrete dust, wings tightly furled.

'Hello, Tolstoy,' whispered the Doctor.

'The serum works. Changed the bat back to normal. But, like you said, the damage to the system caused by the mutation was too severe…' Fynn coughed, and fresh blood poured down his chin. The Doctor tried to take his hand, but Fynn was already clutching something.

'Find her before she changes too.' He pressed it into the Doctor's hand. The data-give. 'Serum's scanned and ready to administer. Three or four doses, I think.' He gripped the Doctor's fingers. 'It had better work. It had better be worth this.'

The Doctor nodded. 'It'll work.'

'Only, I've got to save the world,' Fynn whispered, closing his eyes.

'You know what?' the Doctor murmured. 'You might have done just that.'

Fynn smiled and nodded, shifted in the rubble like a child in bed settling down to peaceful sleep. Then he was gone.

The Doctor gently patted Fynn's hand, and heard a quiet scuffling noise beside him. A glowing point of light was shifting through the cement dust. Adiel's necklace had been crushed by the rubble and the magma traces, freed from the shattered crystals, were moving towards him.

The Doctor stared down at the data-give. It was time to test the solution on himself. 'Turning my blood into mushroom soup. Should make me a fun guy to be with…'

He pressed the device to his arm and hit the transmit switch. A sharp coldness tangled through his veins, spreading up his arm. Then he reached out and touched the glowing speck.

At once he gasped as a burning heat bit into his fingertips. More specks of gold appeared, streaking across the dusty floor, pricking the skin of his other hand.

The Doctor closed his eyes, as a wave of dizziness and nausea passed through him, as sweat started streaming from his pores. The chemical reaction was kicking in, sweeping through his bloodstream, encasing every cell. It was as if his whole body was suffocating from the inside. And at the same time, the magma stuff was singeing its way through his skin, confused after so long in isolation, a few pathetic specks still trying to take control.

He placed his fingers to his temples, focused on the mad rhythm being beaten out by his racing hearts, willed himself to cling on to consciousness.

Then suddenly his eyes were burning. He cried out in pain, scuttled away from Fynn's body, blind, crawling over rock and glass.

When his eyes opened, he saw his dusty reflection, and the gleaming gold around his dark, watering eyes, snaking away through the veins in his face. He closed his eyes and saw crimson shadows, shifting like smoke, felt other thoughts behind his own.

The cloned cell walls had built themselves up around his own, strengthening them – in time he should be able to shrug off the magma effect, just as the fungus had. There was no way of knowing how long before his body chemistry reasserted itself and the cell walls came toppling down. Could he even keep the controlling intelligence at bay for that long?

'Let's find out,' he gasped.

The Doctor shoved the data-give in his pocket, staggered over the debris and ran off down the corridor.

He didn't see the huge, maggoty shape drag itself from its blanket of concrete and dust and come trailing into the ruined lab, sniffing the air, searching…

Outside in the muddy morning light, the Doctor made for the vulture hole. That cave had been under heavy guard and Solomon had been absorbed there – something marked it out for special attention, and he wanted a bit of that himself.

The fighting round there had been and gone by the look of the charred, smoking bones littered all around. Now it raged close to the main entrance to the western caves. He saw golems moving sluggishly, being driven back. The stench was getting worse as the pitiless sun grew stronger.

The gold around his eyes burned with the determination of the animating force, pulsed with its frustration at the inadequacies of the bodies it had taken. The Doctor knew it sensed his difference. It was desperate to control him, not to relinquish this indigestible blood pulsing in his veins. It would send more of itself, he knew that – and he might find himself lost to it.

The Doctor started to climb up the steep crags and foothills.

He peered in through the hole in the lava tube's roof. A golden glow was stirring in the thick shadows, pulsing like a heart. Waiting.

'Coming, Rose,' he said softly.

The Doctor dropped through the hole. He didn't fear the impact of bone on stone, or attack from spiders and scorpions. He knew the true Valnaxi guardian would be waiting to break his fall.

Sure enough it surged out, enveloped him, pushed inside his nose and scorched down his throat. He didn't even have time to shout out. The burning power was engulfing him. Plating his flesh.

Claiming him.

SEVENTEEN

Adiel helped Basel place another of the weird, webbed canvases into the back of the Wurm's transporter. They had loaded up one already – when there was no more room, Faltato had pressed a pincer against a discoloured patch on the shell to send it floating away back down the lava tubes.

'Work slower,' said Basel quietly. 'We need to save some strength for escaping.'

'Escaping where?' she mouthed back. Apparently this cavern was the first he and Rose had found, so he knew a little of the lie of the land.

'That thing took the Doctor's magic screwdriver,' Basel hissed. 'It does loads of things – like it opens up holes in the walls. We might find another way out, another tunnel. If I could get hold of it...'

'Stop plotting,' said Faltato. 'There is nowhere you can go. Nowhere *any* of us can go.'

There was a note of self-pity in Faltato's voice that put Adiel more in mind of men than monsters. His pincers had drooped and he looked quite dejected. She took an uncertain step towards him. 'You can go wherever you want. Can't you?'

'My ship is moored to an asteroid eighty-seven light years from here,' said Faltato gloomily. 'The Wurms dislike independence in those they sponsor.'

Basel was unmoved. 'Think you're mistaking us for people who give a –'

Adiel held up a hand to shush him. 'What's bothering you?' It was weird how quickly you got used to dealing with alien monsters. But then, when they were real-life and real close in your face, it wasn't like you had much choice *other* than to deal with them. 'You think something's wrong, don't you?'

'These artworks… I didn't pay them enough heed before.' Faltato shook his head. 'They should be some of the oldest and most famous of all Valnaxi treasures. But they're not. They are quite ordinary. They all hail from one era. From the middle period of the war.' He shook his pointed head. 'I don't trust this. Any of it.'

And as the next transporter bobbed into view, and as Basel wearily picked up the next painting, Adiel saw Faltato retreat a little way away, a furtive look in his many eyes.

King Ottak watched the loaded transporter hover silently into the cargo hold.

'Treasure,' he sneered. To him it was filthy, worthless stuff, abstract and angular, proof of the absolute weakness and vanity of the Valnaxi. The fools had devoted their lives to their art. Well, he had devoted his to destroying that art, in all its forms.

As usual, he would scatter the pieces to the Five Ends of Empire for the ritual burning and breaking. Only this time the crowds would gather from light years around on the host planet to watch him personally destroy the greatest of all Valnaxi treasures, one after another. The *Lona Venus*... that oh-so-celebrated holy statue in the shape of the Mother Valnaxi... *The Flight of the Valwing*, said to be one of the finest paintings in the cosmos. He would spend days slowly desecrating them, the endless cheers of his people sweet in his sensors.

'Treasure,' he sneered again, louder this time.

More and more these days, in his more reflective moments, Ottak had the niggling feeling that there was something he was missing, something that was going over his head. He peered through his electronically heightened senses at the stuff spilling out from the nearest transporter. He coiled his tail around the figure of a bird and raised it up.

'What secrets do you hold?' Ottak hissed. Then he flexed his muscles and crushed it to dust. 'None. None at all.'

A vibration in the earth beneath him alerted him to someone coming. He turned expectantly – and suddenly a ghostly white head pushed upwards.

It was Korr, burrowing free of the sucking soil. Half of his body had been torn away, trailing ligaments and implants.

'I tried to contact you, sire,' Korr wheezed, 'but the

Valnaxi interference prevented me. Had to burrow here…'

With a low, angry hiss, Ottak swiped at another statue, decapitated a winged figure. 'What happened, Korr?'

'I have located the memory wafers,' he said, spitting them out of his mouth-skin. 'The bipeds betrayed us –'

'– but their machinery is sound,' pronounced Ottak. 'You have done well, Korr. We shall map out the warren and raze all defences, destroy its central systems, empty its treasures and crush them under-belly in the streets of every planet.'

'Their greatest legacy will be lost for all time…' Korr wagged his body-stump from side to side in anticipation. 'My injuries do not trouble me, sire. I wish to fight on.'

'That wish is granted, Korr,' said Ottak without hesitation. 'The soil of this world has been enriched with biped blood and Valnaxi ashes, and we shall taste both in our bodies. We shall battle on and tear the heart from this Valnaxi hellhole. Then we shall ingest it! Then we shall regurgitate it and ingest it again!'

Korr nodded eagerly. Ottak left him there in his own pooling filth and headed for the command mound to fix the biped's machine – before fixing the Valnaxi defences for good.

The Doctor wasn't sure how much time passed in the shadows and bloody backwaters of his mind. But he was dimly aware of his body rising up, moving like a sleepwalker, through the split at the back of the cave, into an empty cavern, trudging through ash. The darkness should have been absolute, but a golden gleam seemed to be lighting his way.

It was coming from his skin. The realisation shocked him into full wakefulness and he put his fingers to his face. It felt cold and hard. His body had begun to turn golem, and his mind was heading the same way.

He had to hold on.

The Doctor pinched his cheek – it was pliable, but dead. He licked his icy golden finger but couldn't taste anything.

'Such a cold finger,' he sang mournfully, the sound soon swallowed up by smoke and shadow. Where was the controlling force? He had to reach Rose before… before…

'This skin is *so* not my colour, by the way,' he complained noisily, trying to wake himself up as much as anyone else. 'I mean, Space City in carnival time it'd go down a storm, but twenty-second-century Africa, come on! Underneath a volcano?' He gave a sharp intake of golden breath, slapped his forehead, felt nothing. '*Underneath* a volcano! How can I have been such a div!'

The data-get scans were taken from Solomon's jeep; they only showed a cross-section through the volcano. They didn't show what was hiding *underneath* it. And even if he could point the D-G down at the ground right now, it only had a range of a kilometre or so. There was as much as *forty* kilometres of crust down there before you reached the mantle…

'And that's where you're hiding, isn't it?' he yelled. 'Deep, deep in the ground, close to the magma that feeds you, and out of the range of any scanning equipment minding your store of treasures. But how do I reach you, then, eh? Since this cave was so well guarded, I'm thinking maybe there's a secret passage, a short cut, a *teleport*. Am I right? Oooh, I bet I'm right.' He wandered around in the dark briefly before losing patience. 'Well? Am I coming to you?' he yelled, 'or are you coming to me?'

The next second, smoky pillars of light, dull as a November dawn, swam faintly into his vision, appeared in front of him. He took a step towards them and they shifted backwards. As he followed after them he felt a tingle like a current through his plated skin.

'Teleport,' he said, grinning to himself. 'I've still got it…'

His surroundings were shifting, growing lighter, brighter. Now suddenly he was in a huge circular space, a giant chimney of flame-red rock stretching upwards into blackness. Four jagged holes were cut at equal intervals into the sides of the natural arena, doorways of some kind – but too dark for him to see what lay beyond.

He was standing on a cushion of air, and beneath him molten lava glubbed and bubbled with powder-flash brightness. He wondered if it was his golem shell protecting him from the heat, or if that was down to the invisible barrier.

Then the glowing shape of the magma-form guardian emerged from the black doorway facing him.

'It's you, is it?' said the Doctor. 'I want to speak to the organ grinder, not his monkey.' The guardian rolled a little closer, and he looked around warily. 'Come on. Where are your mates, then?'

The guardian came to a stop and the Doctor felt a twitch in his mind. 'Oh… No mates. It's just you, isn't it? Must be a whole network of teleportals around so you can check up on the place – you just keep popping up here and there, subdividing to make it *seem* like there's loads of you… Ow!'

The Doctor tailed off as a sibilant whisper swirled through his head like smoke. *Don't resist us. By blocking our control you're upsetting the balance of the defence network. We cannot manipulate our servants. We cannot resist our enemies.*

'Then you'd better give me what I want right now,' snapped the Doctor out loud. 'Rose Tyler.' He took a threatening step towards the magma form. 'You can't harm me any more – but the Wurms can harm *you*, and I'll let them. I don't know why you took her, but I want her back. Now.'

The guardian didn't move.

'Who's in charge here!' the Doctor hollered.

A curtain of smoke seemed to gust away from that same dark doorway as two shiny golden figures shambled into the arena. Misshapen statues of a man and a girl.

'Oh, God,' the Doctor whispered.

The male figure was clearly all that was left of Solomon Nabarr. But it was the sight of the girl that had made the Doctor's hearts stop dead. Her face was a distorted mask, as if the features had formed on a custard skin and been poked about by a child's finger. One cheek, one eye bulged, while the other side seemed to melt down into the fat Schwarzenegger neck. The body was hunched and simian. One arm flapped feebly, clearly broken in two places, while the other was swollen like the misshapen legs. She stood facing him, her distorted features fixed in reproach.

'Rose,' he croaked. 'Oh, Rose, I'm so sorry. I was too late...'

EIGHTEEN

King Ottak started at the sudden sound of clear communication. The ship's scanners burst into full function, scattering the static. In its place came pin-sharp images of the battlefield, courtesy of the cam-flies, their transmissions magically interference-free.

The pictures showed the Valnaxi guardians dropping from the sky, struggling feebly in the ashy murk of the ground. The cams zoomed in eagerly on Ottak's troops blasting the twisted creatures to bits with lasers or cannon-fire, or surging eagerly through the mire towards the doorway to the Valnaxi vaults.

The tech-bugs brought the biped's device to him. They had integrated Korr's memory wafers and powered up the machine. Once the cam-flies had circled the volcano, the layout of the vaults would become clear and a strategy – bold and precise – would be arrived at.

Now Ottak could broadcast his commands over the ship's loudspeakers and be heard. 'Squad One, secure the bipeds' entrance to the easterly tunnels. Squad Two, secure the gateway to the western network. All other units, destroy your enemies where they lie.' He crept over to the internal comms. 'Korr, ready yourself.' He puffed up his soily, segmented chest. 'Soon I will fire the final shots in this long war. The last Valnaxi outpost will stand crushed and its host planet vaporised. It will be soon, Korr.' Ottak smiled inside as he watched his indomitable troops do his work. 'Very soon.'

The Doctor stumbled towards the figures. 'Oh no. Come on... no way,' he said, words almost failing him for once. 'I... Solomon, I'm so sorry... But *Rose*...'

The baleful figures stood watching him.

'Why did you do this?' he shouted up into the rocky arena. 'If they're not fighting Wurms for you up above, why did you need to do this to them down here?'

'*Stop fighting us,*' came the voice. '*There's nothing worth fighting for now. You have lost her. You have lost Rose Tyler.*'

'At least set her body free,' he pleaded. 'Let her be as she was.'

'*Stop fighting us and we will. We promise.*'

The Doctor lowered his head. Then he cocked it to one side. 'We? Hang about. Who's we?' He spun all around. 'Who am I talking to?'

'*There is little time. The Wurms will destroy us and this world you care for. We must defeat them. Surrender yourself to us or we cannot fight.*'

'Stuff that! I'll never surrender!' He looked at the Rose golem, suddenly wary. 'I don't trust this!' He pivoted on one golden foot, shouting into the shadows. 'You're trying to pull a fast one. Who *are* you?'

Suddenly Rose's gleaming skin turned brittle, tore away in flakes of gold. Veins and arteries rose up in her arm, darkened into cracks, split open.

The Doctor stared in alarm – then Solomon hurled one massive golden fist into his chest. Literally. It came away at his wrist as he threw the punch. The Doctor went down in a hail of golden shards as the fist shattered.

He stared up as Rose's lumpy face broke open like a shell.

Or a chrysalis.

Because there was another face behind the crumbling mask. Like an artist's impression of Rose, not quite enough detail, a sketch somehow brought to life. The dead husk of the body peeled away to reveal the slim, muscular figure underneath. It was not hard and golden, nor glowing like magma; the dark-honey flesh looked baby-smooth and flawless, no human complexion could compare. A similar stylised figure was stepping out of the remains of Solomon's golem, but the Doctor's eyes were riveted to the girl and the way she looked at him – at once both so familiar and so strange.

'Rose?' the Doctor whispered.

'No,' said a low, soft voice. 'Not Rose. Rose Tyler is only the template.'

The Doctor sat up. His head felt raw and it hurt to think. 'What do you mean, "template"?'

'The future of the Valnaxi race.' The words came from the male's precisely sculpted lips, but the voice was identical. A tear was running down his cheek.

'Translation pattern now complete. New physical form achieved for both genders. Templates can be discarded.'

'We wished you to surrender peacefully,' said the newly hatched golden Rose, her lips turning down in dismay. 'But we must stop your mental disruption before the Wurms destroy what is left of our army.'

The two figures advanced on the Doctor like golden shades, perfect arms outstretched, perfect hands hooked into claws.

Basel busied himself not just with shifting pictures and figurines but with scoping out Faltato whenever he could, looking for the telltale bulge of the Doctor's device in the monster's flared jacket.

They had moved to the cavern where the bats had attacked Solomon. Unfortunately Faltato had gone straight next door in search of his missing masterworks. He hadn't found them, but he'd found the tunnel the Doctor had opened up – and deliberately caused a cave-in. Not just to stop golems or guardians creeping up behind them, Basel reckoned, but to prove to them there was nowhere they could go.

The screwdriver thing was their only chance. It had driven those bats away from Solomon; it could maybe protect them again. It had to be better than just loading up this freaky treasure till their usefulness was at an end.

Faltato was watching them from a safe distance, as if worried the stuff was about to blow up in their faces.

'Are these from the same period of Valnaxi history

too?' asked Adiel, piling some crockery carefully into the transporter.

'Yes,' he snapped. 'And so are those in the next cavern.'

'That was the last one,' Basel informed him. 'No more after that – just tunnels.'

'But there *must* be more!' Faltato railed, stamping several feet on the floor. 'The *Lona Venus*, *The Flight of the Valwing*… They must be here! Where are they?'

Suddenly a loud, gurgling voice burst from Faltato's communicator, clear as day. 'We have victory over the guardians.'

'King Ottak!' gasped Faltato. 'I – I'm delighted!'

'The routes to the warren are clear and have been scanned and mapped out in full,' he went on. 'After searching for so long, we shall finally seize the Valnaxi masterworks for public desecration. Our hearts, and the hearts of our people, will soon fill with rejoicing. I will be with you shortly.'

'Great!' squeaked Faltato, his pincers flopping due south.

With a final hiss, Ottak broke contact.

'That's it, then,' said Basel weakly. 'They don't need us for protection no more. We're dead.'

Adiel took a deep breath. 'We've got nothing to lose.'

Suddenly she ran off. Faltato turned automatically to stop her – and the second his back was turned, Basel jumped on him. He grabbed hold of the alien round its suited midriff, patting over its pockets for the screwdriver.

'How dare you touch me there!' Faltato spluttered

between high-pitched gasps, then fell writhing to the ground. Adiel doubled back and joined the struggle, but soon cried out as a pincer locked on to her arm, as a tongue lashed out and wound round her neck. Basel found another pincer closing round his throat. He clawed at Faltato's slimy face, jabbing his fingers into his eyes, until two more tongues took hold of his wrists and yanked them so hard he thought both arms might jump out of their sockets.

'Biped savages,' Faltato groaned, legs scrabbling beneath him as he tried to right himself. 'No one crosses me...'

Basel felt the world start to throb into darkness, felt the pincer start to scissor into his neck. They'd blown their last chance. Now it was over.

The Doctor backed away but the golden shades moved with balletic speed and grace to grab him. While the male held him in a bearhug, the female's fingers closed round his throat. She looked oddly unhappy about it, though, staring at her hand as if she did not trust its movements.

Being throttled ought to hurt, the Doctor decided. But it didn't.

'Ha!' he laughed in the female's face. 'Is that all you've got? Can't feel a thing!' The magma form bubbled up to him, surged around his leg, then pulled back uselessly. 'Looks like your guard dog's lost his teeth too. This golden skin makes a warrior out of anything that lives – shame you didn't worry about them ever turning on *you.*' He brought up both legs and planted his feet in the female's stomach, then pushed. That broke her grip on his throat and made the male overbalance, dragging the Doctor down with him. But the female was soon back on the attack. The Doctor rolled backwards out of the way so she stumbled into the male instead.

'New bodies, always tricky getting used to them, isn't it?' the Doctor remarked, eyeing the nearest of the dark doorways. 'Cup of tea helps, I always say. Got any tea? Africa's a good place for tea. We could sit down, have a cup of pure Kenyan, chat things through –'

'Do not fight control!' shouted the male. 'Our enemies are near. We must have defences!'

'And I must have Rose!' he yelled back. 'Solomon too. They're not templates to be discarded, they're *people*. If you will release them and send them out of this place through one of your teleporters… then I'll give myself up to you.' He grinned suddenly. 'And what a catch! I'm spoiling you here.'

The golden figures looked at each other. Then they took a few steps backwards as a golden smoke began to waft across the centre of the arena. Moments later, two golems appeared – the real Rose and Solomon, standing still as statues but not yet mutated.

'Reverse the effect!' he demanded.

'If that were possible,' said the female that had taken Rose as her template, 'we would have done so on *you*.'

'Good point. So it's down to me,' muttered the Doctor, rushing over to them, pulling the data-give from his pocket. He paused for just a second – then gave Rose the first dose, Solomon the second. He held his breath, wondering if it would work, if the magma effect would be driven out by the sudden cellular disruption. Or if all his wild improvising and Fynn's bravery had been for nothing.

'Now you must surrender yourself,' said the male. 'Now you must stop fighting.'

'You said you'd teleport them to safety.'

'There is nowhere safe while you block our network. But they *will* be taken from here.'

The Doctor bit his golden lip and closed his eyes. Darkness pressed in on him almost at once. There was a force in that darkness that wanted to do his thinking for him, wanted to control him. 'Take care, Rose,' he whispered as he let those thoughts crash in and drown him.

NINETEEN

The imperious question roared around the cavern: 'If you are quite finished playing with the bipeds, Faltato?'

For a split second Adiel could only feel overwhelming gratitude as the leathery tongue around her throat slackened its hold and as Basel fell choking to the rocky ground. But then she saw King Ottak and his Wurm hordes squelching into the chamber. Lumps had been pecked out of them, their pink-grey skin was blackened and much of their soil had fallen away, but the mood of bloodlust and elation was unmistakable.

Repulsed by the horror of the scene, she found her attention taken by one who stood out – or rather laid down – from the rest. The giant worm had been chopped in half and was twitching obscenely on a stretcher that looked like the tough green carapace of some enormous insect.

'Your Majesty,' said Faltato, letting Adiel fall panting to the floor. 'I was forced to restrain the bipeds. They attempted to –'

The Wurm king's voice was an icy rasp. 'Where is the *Lona Venus*? Where are the masterworks? I wish to spit on them.'

'Ah.' Faltato grimaced. 'There might be a tiny – *teeny-tiny* – problem there.'

Adiel shivered in the long pause that followed.

'Explain.'

'The, um, bulk of the treasures hail from the most recent eras of Valnaxi history. While still of great merit –'

'Faltato.' Ottak slithered closer. 'Did you, or did you not, identify this warren as the last great Valnaxi stronghold, said to be piled high with the greatest art treasures of all?'

'Based on the visual evidence gathered from the last warren, it was only logical to assume –'

'And have we, or have we not, travelled thousands of light years to secure these promised treasures?'

'I'm sure the treasures will be here *somewhere* and that you will seek them out with your usual aplomb –'

'Cover the exits,' Ottak told his troops.

They squirmed off to obey.

Faltato shifted uneasily. 'King Ottak?'

'If the artworks are not here, then this is not the last of the warrens, as you claimed. It is merely a forgotten outhouse with obsolete defences, of no real worth.' He hissed. 'You are therefore a charlatan or a fool – and I will not tolerate either.'

'The great works *must* be here somewhere,' said Faltato desperately. 'Underground, perhaps. Or – or maybe secreted in the summit –'

'Our scans show there is nothing more!' Ottak insisted. 'I will not be cheated. Squad! Take aim.'

Adiel stared in horror as, with an ominous whirr of servos, the Wurms' stump-guns trained themselves on Faltato. With a yelp he yanked her and Basel back to their feet, held them to him close like a frightened child clutching his teddies.

'Bipeds are soft and fleshy, Faltato,' Ottak went on. 'They will not shield you from us.'

Basel tried weakly to struggle, but Adiel found herself paralysed.

Time seemed to slow to a dread crawl.

Death was coming.

The Doctor opened his eyes but they felt gritty and sore. 'Feeling something! That's nice. Ow! Niceish.' He knelt up and rubbed at his eyes with his hands.

Unless he was very much mistaken, they were fleshy, dirty and definitely non-golden hands.

Breathlessly he rolled up his sleeve, clutched hold of his ankle, scratched his bum and stuck a finger in his ear. 'I'm back!' he shouted. 'I was all ready to give myself up. But your magma gave up on me first! Couldn't handle the cell walls and gave up, just as it did with the 'shroooms! *Ha!*' He whooped for joy and shook his head in disbelief. 'How jammy am I? I'm immune, and now Rose and Solomon will be too! If you have a problem, if no one else can help, call for FUNGUS MAN! He'll be there in the shake of a spore to…' The Doctor tailed off. 'Um, hello?'

He took in his surroundings – not that there was much

to take in. He seemed to be in a deep, dark cave. The only illumination came from veins of faintly glistening light tracing wayward paths over the steep walls. They pulsed gently as if the rock itself was alive.

'You are not Fungus Man.' The voice came out of the darkness, ancient and dry, like the crackle of leaves in a bonfire.

'Um, no,' he admitted. 'I'm the Doctor. Where are Rose and Solomon?'

'They have been taken for teleportation above as you requested.'

'Are they safe?'

'You have risked all our lives.' A pause. 'You are not like the human creatures.'

The Doctor's eyes probed the darkness, trying to see who was talking. 'Have you been peeping?'

'We have scanned you.'

'You're right. But you're not like the human creatures either, are you – so why are you trying to be?' Silence. 'Oh, come on. Shine a little light on the subject.'

The veins of light glowed brighter. Now the Doctor could make out strange, delicate machinery and instrument panels built above rocky perches set high in the rock. The controls seemed powered by thick conduits that snaked down out of sight, presumably into the molten magma below. Clearly this was a centre of operations – or perhaps a throne room. Seven huge ornate structures, halfway between chairs and perches, resolved themselves from out of the gloom. In each, the body of a fierce, bird-like creature with fiery golden scales was propped, immediately familiar from so many statues and paintings in the caves far above. Faint black-gold smoke gusted round the bodies.

The Doctor took a step closer. 'So. The Valnaxi race lives on after all. The last survivors.'

'We are the Council of Valnax,' said the ancient disembodied voice. 'Our bodies are long since dead. Only the intelligence survives.'

'Sentient smoke,' the Doctor murmured. 'And there's no smoke without fire. You did this to yourselves, didn't you?'

'We knew the Wurms would revenge themselves on us.' He turned at the sound of the low growl to find the female in Rose's image standing just behind him. 'Knew that they would scour the universe for all traces of our civilisation, to steal our art and treasures.'

'And we knew that we could never return home.' The male based on Solomon had also stepped out from the darkness. 'That we faced eternal persecution.'

'So the chosen few hid themselves away down here,' the Doctor surmised.

'Though we lack flesh, we are many thousands,' the old voice said. 'Though most choose to lie sleeping until they have a future to wake to.'

'Waiting for the heat to die down under a volcano!' The Doctor grinned. 'That's brilliantly twisted. Ha, ha, ha! That's genius!'

'The planet's mantle sustains our systems,' came the aged whisper. 'And fresh eruptions hid all traces of our arrival.'

'Apart from a tektite or two.' The Doctor took a step closer to the thrones. 'But you knew the Wurms would find you some day. In fact, you *wanted* them to. You didn't leave those riddles and clues to the whereabouts of each successive warren for your descendants to find, 'cause your descendants are down here with you.' He lowered his voice. 'You set a trap, didn't you? A long, slow trap.'

'The Wurms are brutally efficient but unimaginative,' came the old, crackling voice. 'By defending each warren in the same way, we have conditioned their responses.'

'Each time,' said the female, 'they must scout the land, fight the guardians and the ranks of local sentries –'

'People and animals,' said the Doctor savagely, 'living creatures whose purpose you perverted and pressganged into perpetuating this pathetic war.' He paused. 'Blimey, what a lot of p's! Can't you give p's a chance?'

'The Wurms thrive on conflict,' said the male. 'It was important to satisfy their desire for violence, to lead them onwards.'

'So they battle their way through to a deactivation plaque and shut down the auto-defences,' the Doctor concluded. 'Then they ransack the warrens to their heart's content and pick up the clues pointing them on to the *next* little treasure trove. But here – for the one and only time – it's different.'

'The deactivation plaques respond only to the touch of flesh. The plaque far above is a fake, a decoration. It conceals a genetic sampler designed to extract DNA, life essence and psychic energy at first touch. Everything we need to reformat our race from a new template.'

'Why?'

'If the Valnaxi are ever to return to our home world and know peace, we need new identities. A new form.' The smoke swirled in a tight, impatient motion. 'The form of our tormentors.'

'The *Wurms?*' The Doctor stared in consternation. 'Why d'you wanna look like Wurms?'

'External appearances are irrelevant,' said the female. 'As artists we see through them to perceive the truth of things.'

'What kind of an answer's that?' the Doctor complained. 'And why such an elaborate scheme? Surely you must have had Wurm prisoners you could have taken as templates?'

The smoke darkened a touch. 'Wurms disintegrate themselves rather than remain prisoners. In any case, in the war time such technology did not exist. Science does not come easily to our race. It took many years to refine the process.' A pause, then the voice continued more sadly, 'We overestimated our enemies' abilities – believed the Wurms would find our warren here far, far sooner. We thought, perhaps, 300 years…'

'And instead you've been stuck here for 2,000.' The Doctor whistled. 'I'm sorry. I really am. No offence, but as scientists and master planners you lot make very good artists.'

'It is for our art we have done this,' came the dry old voice. 'Our planet is home to a binding force, an energy – the wellspring of our creativity.'

'Yes, I know.'

'And away from the homelands, we cannot create,' the voice went on. 'We have no art. No function, no purpose. Our most ancient and valuable masterworks are hidden away in vaults here, and we wait with them. Until the day we can return to create new and better works.'

'Return?' The Doctor stared at the bodies on their thrones. 'So. You wanted to look like Wurms so you could fit in back home…'

'They infest our world but cannot destroy the binding force. It waits there for us. It calls to us.' A pause. 'We are so little without it. We fought so hard and for so long to preserve it. Now, if the only way we are able to commune with it is to live among our conquerors in secret, then so be it.'

'Only it's all gone wrong, hasn't it?' said the Doctor. ''Cause here you are, all arms and legs. After all those centuries, the Wurms didn't make it to the bogus deactivation plaque first, did they?' He shook his head sadly at the gleaming, stylised figures. 'Solomon did!'

As she stared down the barrels of two dozen cannons, Adiel knew she should have been terrified. But there were too many questions crowding her head. How had her parents felt, looking back at the end of *their* lives? How afraid had they been? What had even happened to them? She'd spent so long clinging to the same questions, and with all she'd found out she was still no nearer an answer. And now, as she faced the taking of her own life, she realised that it didn't matter. The answers to those questions would change nothing. She would never stop missing her mum and dad, never stop loving them, never stop wanting to make them proud.

And as the guns finished clicking into position, fear finally bit at her. And in its teeth came the certainty that her mum and dad would have fought to stay alive, done anything, *tried* anything.

She would fight too.

'Any last words, Faltato?' the Wurm king enquired mockingly.

'None come to mind,' said Faltato faintly. 'Oh, hang on...'

Adiel realised something was digging into her back. Something in Faltato's breast pocket that Basel must have overlooked. A little jolt of hope went through her and she twisted in Faltato's grip. 'Don't make me look at them!' she wailed, pressing herself up against him and dipping into the pocket. Her fingers closed on a slim tube.

'King Ottak,' said Faltato wretchedly, 'allow me to speak to my fellows at the Hadropilatic Fellowship. Let them double-check my findings and prove to you –'

Discreetly she pulled out the tube, reached over and pressed it into Basel's hand. He started, looked at her. Grinned and nodded.

Ottak hissed like an air brake. 'I tire of your final words, Faltato.'

('Can you work it?' Adiel asked Basel.)

'Let us revel in your final screams instead!'

('I can die trying,' he whispered.)

Faltato's nerve finally broke and he launched into a

desperate stumbling run, dragging his human shield with him.

'Aim your weapons!' Ottak roared to his troops.

Basel raised the thin little tube. A blue glow of power buzzed from its tip. Adiel waited, breath baited.

But all that happened was the Wurm on the stretcher yelped as his floating stretcher whizzed off as if jerked on a string and smashed into the cavern wall, before capsizing over the patient.

'Korr!' Ottak hissed. 'Biped scum, your blood shall enrich my soil for this!'

Basel looked at Adiel helplessly – then Faltato slipped and collapsed, dragging them down with him. Adiel cringed as her face fell against his – it was like nuzzling a big rotten vegetable.

'Destroy them all!' roared Ottak.

But then Adiel blinked as a skein of golden smoke drifted into sight right in front of them. Two gleaming figures began to form there.

'Golems!' shouted Basel.

Adiel closed her eyes. The Wurms opened fire.

The Doctor stared half-disgusted, half-pityingly at the blank faces of the Valnaxi-humans. 'What a cods-up,' he said. 'Lying dormant all this time, you didn't realise the humans had developed, that they'd been digging out the volcano and weakened the caverns – exposing the plaque too soon. Solomon found it, touched it and your systems took *his* DNA, life essence and psychic energy...' He nodded, growing excited. 'Maybe that's why you didn't see him as a threat till he brought the roof crashing down on the plaque and smashed it! And so now you can't steal the Wurms' identities. They're gonna loot the place and push off and torch the whole planet, and while you may survive way down here, you're stuck as humans – and ohhhhh boy are you ever gonna stand out like sore thumbs on your home world looking like *that*...'

He tailed off, expecting confirmation, or angry denial – *something*. But the throne room stayed silent. The smoke hung in an almost solid curtain just ahead of him. The male and the female watched him closely.

'Um, it's good of you to tell me all this by the way,' he said quickly. 'But – call me paranoid, I'm suddenly wondering why. Why?'

The silence, the watching, went on. Then suddenly the magma guardian blazed threateningly into the throne room.

'Oh, I get it,' said the Doctor. 'You've been waiting for my cells to revert, haven't you? So you can make me into one of your golems.'

The female looked at him almost sadly. 'Yes.'

He pulled a face. 'And... I'm guessing my immunity's worn off?'

The male nodded.

'Whoops,' said the Doctor, as the magma form surged towards him.

TWENTY

Eyes tight shut, Adiel listened to the squelch of the Wurm cannons, blast after blast, and wondered how come she was still alive. But only when she felt human hands gripping her own did she open her eyes.

Solomon was crouching protectively over her, no longer golden, just the same as he had always been.

'I – I thought you were dead,' she stammered.

'There's still time,' he said grimly, dragging her up. 'Come on. *Move.*'

Adiel saw in a moment that Faltato was no longer prime target, with or without his human shield. The Wurms had opened fire on the storm of bats and vultures that had soundlessly swooped into the chamber to attack, and the packs of misshapen dogs and hyenas that now came snapping and howling to join the fray. The Wurm guarding the jagged entrance to the next chamber had left his post to take part in the fighting, and Adiel realised that Rose was leading Basel to shelter there. Faltato was already disappearing through the slit in the stone.

'Where did you appear from?' Adiel shouted over another deafening volley of shots as they pushed through into the next chamber.

'Out of thin air, I think,' said Rose. She looked pale and woozy, trying to hold Basel upright while holding it together herself. Adiel took him off her hands and they all collapsed behind an enormous Valnaxi sculpture – where Faltato was waiting.

'Out of thin air, indeed.' Faltato sniffed. 'You were sent through a matter transporter.'

'It was amazing,' said Basel, kissing Rose before throwing his arms round Solomon. 'They came through this smoky yellow light, all gold and golem-y – then it just wore off and they were normal.'

'We weren't regular golems,' said Rose, eyes closed, fingers pressing against her face. 'We were, like, golems deluxe.'

'They wanted something else from us,' Solomon agreed. 'And I guess they must have taken it.'

Faltato clearly wasn't impressed. 'From the timing, I'd say they sent you through to distract Ottak's forces while their guardian drones attacked from the rear. Though I don't see why the drones were playing dead...'

'Something the Doctor did,' said Rose. 'He was down there, blocking their golem control.'

The alien groaned. 'I might have known he'd be behind it.'

'I could see you all,' said Solomon distantly. 'The moment I was taken, it was like I was part of some greater mind... Like that mind was listening to *me*. I did my best to keep those golden creatures away from you. But when I knew whatever was holding me needed a female for study, I…' He looked between Adiel and Rose, awkward and shamefaced. 'I couldn't let Adiel…'

'It's OK,' Rose said kindly. 'She's your mate. You only just met me.'

'Listen to me.' Faltato's five eyes narrowed at Solomon and Rose. 'You've been held in a hidden Valnaxi stronghold, haven't you? How many Valnaxi are there?'

'I dunno,' said Rose. 'It all gets blurry. There were these voices in my head… eyes inside my body.' She frowned, rubbing at her arm. 'The Doctor got us back. He must still be down there. They've got him!'

'Excellent,' Faltato declared triumphantly. 'Not just a hidden Valnaxi stronghold, but a populated one! What better to get a thug-king like Ottak back onside than the chance to personally slaughter the last of his bitterest enemies?'

'The gunfire's stopped,' Solomon hissed.

'But I'm just getting started.' Before anyone could react, Faltato jumped up, grabbed hold of Rose and half-dragged, half-carried her over towards the entrance to the Wurm-infested cavern.

'No need to stop the chat,' said the Doctor, springing aside as the magma form lashed out a molten tendril. 'Tell me why you had to kidnap Solomon if you already had his genetic material from the plaque?'

No answer. The incandescent blob came rolling towards him again.

'All right, let's see if I can guess.' He took a running jump up and over the guardian, felt the heat of its flickering form through the soles of his sneakers. 'Obvious answer, you didn't get *enough* material from him. He probably barely touched your silly plaque. It's not like he was trying to deactivate anything, was it?' He backed away through the stinging curtain of smoke, tried not to choke. 'So you needed a proper study – it's not ideal, but if this is the form you're gonna be stuck in, you want to make the best of things. You don't want to be lumbering about all misshapen like your mutant golems up there – it's fine for the cannon fodder, but not very pretty, not very *artistic*…'

The male and the female advanced on him.

'But you had Solomon, so why take Rose too?' The Doctor leapt lightly up on to one of the throne-perches, careful not to crush the ancient, burnished body underfoot. 'And why do you want me so badly you can't just kill me?'

'Wurms are capable of reproducing themselves independently by the hundreds,' said the bitter, crackling voice. 'Solomon is a male. Our study of male and female forms shows us that only the mature female of the species is equipped to grow offspring.'

'*Vive la différence*, eh?' He vaulted over the high back of the throne as the blob surged up to get him. 'Ever met the French, by the way? Never mind. So – you tried to copy Rose, kept her and Solomon in some kind of stasis so they wouldn't mutate till you'd got your templates right. You're getting closer, but still not quite there, are you?'

'Human reproduction is clumsy and inefficient,' the voice went on. 'It would take centuries to grow enough bodies to sustain our sleeping people. But now we have a detailed genetic blueprint of the human form we can assimilate them without mutation, replace their minds with our own – in a fraction of the time.'

As the old voice spoke, the male appeared at the other end of the line of thrones, blocking the Doctor's retreat. 'That is why we must stop the Wurms destroying this planet. Why they must die here.'

'We can improve humans,' the voice went on. 'Style them. Refashion them in this image.'

'They're not just bodies, clay for you to mould like you do your golems,' the Doctor shouted. 'They're people. Individuals. Brilliant, wonderful *individual* individuals, leading lives of their own.'

'We have sensed your intimate knowledge of this planet and its peoples,' said the dry and dusty voice. 'It will be of great assistance to us as we move to take control of Earth.'

'We will rule over the surplus humans and make armies from them,' said the male. 'Armies that will finally drive out the Wurms from our home world.'

'We are desperate,' said the female softly, almost apologetic. 'We must return. It has been so long –'

'I'll never help you,' the Doctor swore. 'I'll *stop* you.'

The seething magma form billowed over the top of the throne beside him, ready to engulf him.

The Doctor flinched from the ferocity of the creature's heat and his back slammed against the wall. With sudden inspiration he grabbed hold of one of the conduits snaking up to the machinery set high in the walls. As the male and the female rushed to get him, as the magma surged forwards, he hauled himself up and out of reach, scaling the rock like a seasoned climber.

'There can be no escape, Doctor,' said the female.

He glared down at the creatures gathering to get him, pressed his head against the hot, barren rock-face and did his best to convince himself she wasn't right.

Rose struggled desperately in Faltato's grip. Her body felt like it had been put through a blender, every nerve and muscle was frayed, but no way was she giving up and hanging limp in the grip of the tongue-meister's pincers.

'Get off her!' Basel shouted, and he, Adiel and Solomon began to follow.

But Faltato cracked out five tongues at once like whips. 'Keep back!' he warned them.

As he pushed Rose up against the split in the rock, she guessed by the smoking bones lying around that the Wurms had come out victorious against Golden Bambi's evil animal army. The big Wurm wearing a crown had to be their king, and the others were gathered round him as he operated a data-get with the help of some robotic probes sticking out of his stumpy shoulders.

'Hear me, Ottak!' Faltato shouted. 'There is a secret Valnaxi lair hidden somewhere close by, reachable only by teleport. That's where you'll find the masterworks – and the last of the Valnaxi!'

King Ottak casually fired a laser bolt in their direction

and Rose flinched as her face was peppered with shrapnel. 'I witnessed the warp-hole opening with my own senses.'

'They've been living on in secret all this time!' Faltato cried desperately. 'I can help you get to them.'

'I shall investigate without your aid.' A large blue centipede crawled up the Wurm's muddy body and clung to the side of his head, as if it was whispering in an invisible ear. 'My tech-bugs have recorded the warp-hole's energy signature.'

'But –'

'Korr, with your stretcher's motive systems damaged, you cannot accompany us,' said Ottak. 'Be revenged on Faltato and all his blithering bipeds instead, and welcome us upon our return.'

'May your victory be wondrous, King Ottak,' grunted Korr. Then he turned his attention to Faltato and Rose.

Rose felt sick as she watched him struggle towards them. He was only half the Wurm the others were, but no less terrifying – like an enormous maggot whose body ended in an open wound, mechanical innards trailing from the severed flesh.

As Korr fired his gun at them, Faltato quickly ducked away from the split in the rock.

'Couldn't keep your mouth shut, could you?' said Rose crossly, pulling herself free of his grip.

'There's no way out,' hissed Adiel. 'Faltato blocked it off.'

'How was I to know?' the monster moaned.

Rose crept back to the hole in the wall, peered out.

'Squad!' Ottak was commanding. 'Set all comm-link implants to frequency seven-zero-nine-gamma and broadcast at volume ten. We will force the warp-hole to reopen.'

Then she saw Korr slither back into view from behind the Wurm transporter. He fired his weapon and she ducked back inside as a bolt of energy missed her head by millimetres.

'It's just him we've got to deal with,' she said. 'The others are gonna go through that teleport thing. I've got to get after them.'

Basel frowned. 'You're crazy!'

'I told you, the Doctor must still be down there. He needs our help! So we're gonna need a plan…' Rose looked up at the spindly stalactites in the cavern roof and then smiled at Faltato. 'And someone who's good with his tongue.'

The Doctor clung on to his conduit while the Valnaxi debated below.

'Our final attempt to destroy the Wurms has failed,' hissed the disembodied Valnaxi voice. 'Sending through the human male and female failed to distract King Ottak. The last of the drones has been destroyed.'

'Alert!' croaked a new voice, wavering and grave. 'Teleport is activating. The Wurms have found the trigger frequency.'

'They have found *us*,' cried the female.

A horrible squelching, squashing noise carried from outside the throne room as the Wurms moved forwards.

'Attack!' bellowed the familiar voice of King Ottak. 'Kill everyone. Destroy everything. *Attack!*'

'Everyone set?' Rose hissed, clutching the sonic screwdriver tight in her hand.

'This is taking liberties,' Faltato complained.

The alien was perched on a high ledge opposite the entrance to the Wurm cavern. He had played out a record-breaking six of his tongues, wrapping them round stalactites poking down from the dark ceiling, and Solomon and Adiel were standing right behind him, holding him in position. In turn, Faltato was using all four pincers to hold on to Basel, clutching him like a dad might hold on to his son on a rollercoaster ride.

Rose checked Korr was on course. 'He's almost here,' she reported, tensing herself to give the signal.

'Submit!' Korr gurgled, wriggling closer and closer to the split in the rock. 'Submit and I shall kill you quickly. There is nothing you can do to stop me.'

'Yeah?' murmured Rose, pressing herself back against the cave wall as she signalled across to the others – *now*!

Solomon and Adiel launched Faltato from the ledge. He swung from his tongues, slackening some while tightening up others, guiding himself through the air. Basel stayed snug in the grip of Faltato's pincers, holding both his legs out in front of him.

The moment Korr pushed his armoured head in through the entrance to the cavern, Rose hit the screwdriver. Distracted by the blue light, the Wurm turned – and was kicked so hard in the face by Basel's big clodhoppers, his truncated body did somersaults through the air. He landed with a wet, greasy splat on his back on a rocky slope and lay still.

Faltato released his tongues and flolloped down in the middle of the cavern, his dainty legs splaying everywhere.

'We did it!' Basel shouted, rolling away from him.

'How undignified,' Faltato complained.

'Now get out of here, all of you!' Rose shouted at them. She was already sprinting towards the pall of golden smoke, which still lingered in mid-air in the centre of the cavern.

'You can't just run in there,' Adiel shouted after her.

'You've got no cover, no protection,' Basel added.

Rose skidded to a halt beside the floating egg-shaped transporter. He was right. What the hell could she do? Then, mind racing, she took in the assortment of canvases and statues piled up inside the transport.

And a slow smile spread over her face.

Still clinging on, the Doctor watched helplessly as Ottak led a squad of twenty Wurms straight into the throne room.

'Fight!' the ancient voice crackled round the room. 'Or all is lost.'

At once, the magma guardian split itself into four smaller blobs and rolled forwards to attack. Three Wurms were turned into golden statues – only to be blasted by their fellow troopers a moment later. One of the magma blobs wasn't quite swift enough on the attack and found itself half-buried in clods of thick mud, then devoured by the teeming insects.

The male and the female were crouching behind the thrones out of sight, looking terrified. And with good reason. Ottak was pushing through his writhing warriors, transfixed by the bodies on the thrones.

'Valnaxi!' the king roared. 'Surrender your treasures to me!'

Then one of the Wurms reared up, saw the Doctor hanging there, shot a laser bolt in his direction.

'Oi!' the Doctor complained, ducking aside. 'I'm neutral in all this.'

The Wurm fired again and burned through the conduit beneath the Doctor's foot. Thick, white-hot magma spurted from the hole in the pipe, spattering down on the battling throng. Wurms screamed as their soil sizzled, while the guardians seemed to revel in the downpour.

Grimly, the Doctor climbed higher up the damaged conduit towards the rocky roof, past various panels in the wall. 'Guidance and cruise systems,' he noted, interested despite himself. 'Not just a throne room, then – a flight deck!' He glanced behind him – and saw on the wall directly opposite, above the entrance to the throne room, that one gleaming panel was hugging the stone. 'Must be the propulsion systems.' Another bolt of laser fire buzzed past him and the Doctor looked down at the Wurms crossly. 'Don't you ever learn?'

Clearly they didn't, as two of them fired again, nearly taking his head off. Perhaps he could put their single-minded belligerence down to their not having had a positive role model. For beneath them, boiling lava was raining down on King Ottak, scorching skin and soil alike, but he seemed oblivious to anything except crowing over the remains of the Valnaxi Council.

'Beg for your lives!' he commanded, spitting jet after jet of black bile at the bodies. 'In the name of the five curves of the Wurm Empire, I kill you!'

'You can never kill us,' boomed the disembodied voice.

But the king had already opened fire with his laser, blasting bolt after bolt into the great bronzed bodies, scorching them, destroying them. 'Die!' he wailed madly, in the downpour of lava. 'I shall ingest your blood, excrete it into my finest soil and ingest it again! Diiiiiiie!'

'Stop this!' the Doctor shouted down, over the pandemonium. 'Ottak, you don't need to...'

But as if fired up by the lava, two of the guardians were flowing towards him. Blasted full of mud and maggots, one broke into smaller balls to minimise the damage. But the other hurled itself on to Ottak's back.

The Wurm king howled with pain as the plating spread over his segmented skin. But like a monster possessed he kept beating his blackened head down upon the remnants of the bodies again and again, swiping scraps of their ancient flesh to the floor and grinding them against his belly. The Doctor looked away as the Wurm's screams stopped dead. The magma might have consumed his body, but Ottak's mind had been consumed by his blind hatred long ago.

The other Wurms were fighting on, the male and the

female their targets now. The Doctor stared down helplessly – then suddenly remembered the explosive phial he'd cooked up back in Fynn's lab. He reached in his pocket, pulled it out.

He only had the one shot – what to do with it?

Then suddenly a Wurm transporter came racing through the throne room's entrance like a bat into hell. It sent Wurms scattering like skittles, squashing a magma form as it landed square on top of it.

Then the hatch sprang open to reveal a very familiar pilot.

'Rose!' the Doctor yelled, and he laughed with delight. 'What d'you think you're doing?'

'Rescuing you,' she shouted back, kicking a Wurm cannon aside and hurling the sonic screwdriver up to him. 'Someone's got to save the day!'

'How right you are.' He stuck the phial between his teeth, caught the sonic in his left hand, pulled free a conduit snaking up to the roof with his right.

Then he leaned back, spat the phial at the guidance controls and launched himself into space, gripping the thick cable. The control panel exploded noisily as he swung out over the smoking chaos of battle below, clear across the throne room, before throwing himself at the golden panel. He gasped, clinging on with one hand to a large gleaming lever. 'Propulsion units, propulsion units…' He started tracing the circuit – through a sudden golden smokescreen.

'What are you doing?' hissed the accusing, crackling voice in his ears.

'As a matter of fact…' The Doctor grinned wildly, gave two short bursts on the sonic and triggered the controls. 'I'm taking off.'

Then he dropped down below, landing squarely on top of the hovering transporter which Rose had steered beneath him.

'Out of here!' he shouted, dodging the mud-splat of a Wurm cannon as the throne room started to shake. The bubble lurched off and he clutched hold of the translucent shell to stop himself slipping.

Golden shapes were flitting beneath the surface.

'Rose?' the Doctor yelled in alarm. The bubble came to a halt in the middle of the arena he'd first arrived in – and as the hatch swung open, he saw that the male and the female were curled up inside, together with Rose.

The Doctor jumped down and grabbed her, pulled her away from the golden couple. 'You OK?'

She nodded shakily. 'Couldn't stop them dumping the artwork and coming aboard.' She lowered her voice. 'That one looks like me.'

'You reckon?' He slipped a protective arm round her. 'Not a patch.'

A vibration had started up. Through the cushion of air they stood on, the Doctor could see the lava churning and slopping far below.

'You have activated the drive systems,' said the male calmly. 'Initiated launch sequence.'

'I had to,' said the Doctor. 'This is your war. Not Earth's. Whoever wins or loses, this planet's people will be destroyed.'

Rose smiled at him. 'So you're forcing a draw?'

He nodded as the arena shook with the blast of some colossal explosion deep beneath them. 'The ship's gonna take off. And it'll take a fair-sized chunk of this volcano with it.'

'Then we've got to get out of here,' said Rose. 'Where's the teleport?'

'Non-functioning,' the male responded. 'The power feeds were damaged in the fighting.'

'Our ship has lain here, hidden for thousands of years, insinuating itself into the rock,' the female added. 'With the drives at less than full power, we could be torn apart.'

'I had to make the call,' said the Doctor sadly. 'Everyone on this planet, or us.'

'Us?' said Rose quietly.

''Fraid so,' he said, as the vibrations worsened around them and dust and debris began to trickle from the distant ceiling. 'Even if we survive the take-off, we'll be trapped here for the rest of our lives.'

TWENTY-ONE

Rose stared at the Doctor as the thought of being stuck here for ever began to sink in to her shellshocked mind. 'The rest of our lives,' she echoed.

'That will not be long,' rasped a battle-scarred Wurm behind them.

She heard a whirr of gears as its gun attachment extended – then the buzz of the sonic screwdriver. The Wurm screeched as its gun started to jerk about, as probes extended from its shoulder and a loud squeal of feedback blasted from the speakers in its comms helmet.

'What are you doing?' asked the male.

'Turning his battle implants up to the max,' said the Doctor coldly. 'Should put him out for a while.'

But Rose was staring the other way as a faint trail of golden light appeared like stardust. 'Doctor, the teleport!' she shouted, half-delighted, half-terrified she was dreaming. 'The Wurms used their communicators to open it, boosted the frequencies or something.'

'And now it's opening for us!' The Doctor adjusted the

sonic's settings. 'Let's make it *wide* open.'

The Wurm gave an excited yelp and started to twist itself into knots, its probes smoking, its sensors going fruit loops as the Doctor boosted the implants further and the golden spiral of smoke grew brighter.

'Through you go, quick!' shouted the Doctor, bundling Rose towards it. 'Before he short-circuits.'

'Not without you!' She grabbed his hand and dragged him after her.

They vanished into the golden void –

And emerged again in the silent, deserted cavern.

The Doctor looked almost comically startled and Rose stared round in disbelief. 'We made it,' she breathed. 'We actually made it!'

'Yes,' said her golden double, 'we did.'

She was standing just behind them with the golden Solomon.

'Rats from a sinking ship?' the Doctor enquired. 'Or from one ready to take off and never come back?' He squared up to them. 'I blew up your navigation systems. I couldn't allow the Valnaxi to fly straight back here and butcher all humanity into their image.'

'We know what you did,' said the golden Solomon. 'That is why we two choose to remain on Earth.'

'After so many empty centuries clutching at schemes and dreams,' breathed Rose's golden double, 'we *must* taste life again – in any form.'

A vast tremor tore through the cavern. 'If we hang around here you won't be tasting it for long,' the Doctor shouted.

'Let's get out of here,' Rose agreed.

'Wait!' The Doctor had seen Korr, lying on the slope, and raced to check on him. 'He's injured, but still alive.' He pointed to an upturned green shell. 'Get that stretcher.'

Another tremor nearly knocked them off their feet. Rose staggered over to the stretcher. 'Give me a hand, then!'

'Leave it to die,' hissed the Solomon-thing.

'Point one,' said the Doctor sternly, 'the only viable shelter round here is the Wurm ship – and Korr can get us inside. Point two – show this kind of attitude to intelligent life and I'll never let you stay here on Earth.'

'We do not need you to grant us permission.'

The coldness in the Doctor's smile made Rose shiver. 'Yes. You do.'

The whole cavern shook again. Stalactites started to drop down from the ceiling like deadly darts. The Valnaxi quickly took the stretcher from her and carried it easily to Korr's side. They hesitated for a few moments. Then they loaded the injured Wurm aboard and raised the stretcher.

'Good.' The Doctor grinned. 'Well, don't just stand about. Haven't you noticed this whole place is falling down around our ears? *Run!*'

'What's happening?' Basel yelled as Solomon, Adiel and Faltato followed him out of the lava tubes and into the dusty daylight. The ground was shaking so hard, he could imagine the hot white sky was about to fall in on them. 'Is the volcano erupting?'

'Feels more like a spaceship's getting ready to take off out from the volcano – dredging up who knows what as it goes.' Faltato went clip-clopping off on his dainty legs. 'You do what you like, but I'm heading for the Wurm ship. It's got a force-field.'

Solomon frowned. 'A what?'

'It'll keep us safe if we get inside,' Adiel panted. 'You want to be out here when the top blows off that volcano? Come on. I don't trust Faltato not to shut us out if he gets there first.'

The monster snickered. 'Perhaps you're not such a stupid biped after all.'

Together they raced up to the huge, slimy ship, sat upon its mountain of stinking mud. And then Basel stopped and stared. 'Solomon… look.'

Vivid green shoots were protruding everywhere from the soil, strong and fat and fleshy.

'It's the corn-vera crop,' Solomon breathed. 'Growing like wildfire.'

'But this muck only came down last night,' said Basel. 'It must be, like, *super*-fertile!'

'Come *on*,' Adiel urged them, struggling up the trembling mud pile while Faltato raced ahead. 'Hang around out here and it won't be corn-vera we're pushing up, it'll be daisies!'

Rose raced on through the shaking tunnels, clutching the Doctor's hand. It was like the rock itself was grinding and screaming around them, and the air was crimson and thick with choking, blinding dust.

'The launch sequence is almost completed,' the male said grimly, staggering into the wall and almost dropping his end of Korr's stretcher.

'What's gonna happen if the ship takes off?' Rose asked.

'The ship's a champagne cork and the volcano's the bottle,' said the Doctor, still dragging her along. 'The bottle's shaking, surrounding lava's fizzing up and the cork's gonna pop, go shooting out, right into space. Whoooosh!' He laughed out loud. 'That's if there's enough power getting through to the drive systems.'

Rose was too busy choking on dust to join in the laughter. 'And if there isn't?'

'The whole bottle explodes. Very, very messily.' He tugged her along more urgently. 'Now, save your breath and keep running. Reaching the Wurm ship's our only chance!'

The four of them pushed on with the unconscious Wurm. Rose half-wished she was out of it too. With every step she imagined the ground breaking up beneath her, or the roof falling in. It was stiflingly hot and, with diabolic red lights glaring from the walls, it felt as if they were charging through hell.

At last they reached the exit doors and came out into open air. The rotten-egg stench of sulphur made Rose want to retch. She could see a poisonous yellow cloud belching from the spout of the volcano.

'It's going to erupt!' she shouted, fear rooting her to the spot.

'The Wurm ship,' the Doctor bellowed. 'Come *on*.'

Rose forced herself into action, running alongside the golden couple, Korr on his stretcher, the Doctor leading the way up the sticky, muddy slope towards the waiting spaceship. But in her heart she already knew it was too late.

There was an ear-splitting boom as the air itself seemed to split apart. Rose fell flat on her face in the thick, muddy slime, scrabbled at green shoots to pull herself up, twisted round to see the top of the volcano *explode*. A long, twisting shard of burnished metal burst out: the Valnaxi spaceship, like an arrow shot into the stars. But the thick blanket of burning, white-hot debris that had burst out with it was already falling back to Earth.

Rose realised that it would rain down right on top of them.

She scrabbled up the muddy slope, into the Doctor's arms. He bent over her, shielding her body with his own.

But the debris never hit.

It showered down, but then bounced and scattered and burned up a good ten metres from the ground, as if an invisible umbrella had opened over them to absorb the deadly rain.

'Ha-haaaa!' whooped the Doctor. 'Neutronic partition!'

'I'm glad you got to the mud slopes in time,' Adiel called from a hatch in the rubbery belly of the ship. 'We saw you coming, but it seems that's as far as the force-field extends.'

The Doctor looked impressed. 'You worked out the controls?'

'We were able to twist Faltato's arms on your behalf. All four of them.'

'Thanks,' said Rose, closing her eyes. 'Doctor, we made it!'

'And so did they,' he murmured, staring up at the Valnaxi ship, now little more than a speck disappearing into the ashen sky.

Rose looked at him. 'They'll go on fighting, won't they?'

He shrugged. 'Who knows? If the situation's tight enough, maybe they'll call a truce. But fingers crossed, they won't ever return. I'll wipe the memory of the flight systems on Korr's ship too, save any reprisals against humanity...'

Adiel had moved a little way down the slope. 'You going to introduce us to your friends?'

The male and the female looked at the Doctor.

'Don't know who you mean,' he said lightly. 'There's no one here. No one I need to worry about.' He looked at them both, stared deep into their golden eyes. 'Is there?'

Slowly they smiled and shook their heads.

The Doctor took one end of Korr's stretcher and gestured that Rose should take the other. They carried him up the sticky slope.

Rose glanced back when they'd reached the ship. But the golden couple had already gone.

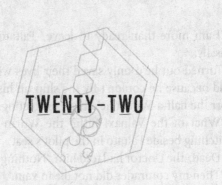

TWENTY-TWO

They couldn't leave till the Wurms' landing-site muck was cleared, since the TARDIS lay buried beneath it. It had taken two days already for the returning workers to get the mountain down as far as they had.

With a twinge of guilt – a small one, mind, after what she'd been through lately – Rose watched the staff beavering away from the comfort of the air-conditioned common room, shifting the muck and storing it out of sight in the surviving lava tubes. She half-smiled. The Doctor didn't like to hang around and deal with the fallout of their adventures, but when the fallout was this big and this smelly there wasn't a lot he could do.

Luckily there had been plenty of loose ends to tie up.

When the Valnaxi ship had crashed out of Mount Tarsus, with all the smoke and tremors the world and his wife assumed the volcano had erupted.

'We'll have aid workers turning up in droves,' the Doctor had moaned. 'Can't have them finding a Wurm warship. It's got to go.'

'I am more than ready to leave,' Faltato had replied prissily.

Turned out he'd only saved their lives with the force-field because he couldn't fly the ship on his own. It was Korr the half-a-Wurm he'd been protecting.

'What of the Valnaxi filth?' the Wurm had snarled, twitching beside Faltato in the pilot's seat.

'Dead,' the Doctor had told him. 'Nothing left of them.'

'Then my comrades did not die in vain.'

The Doctor had stared down at him then, suddenly looking so tired. 'Oh… push off.'

'Hello, Rose.' Adiel breezed into the room, grabbed a drink from the fridge.

'Hello, Acting Director,' Rose replied.

Adiel looked tired as hell but as happy as someone who'd been there and come back. 'The Doctor was right. That muck is a gift. It's like a dream. Too much to hope for.'

Rose grinned. 'You've run your tests and simulations and that?'

'Anything grows in it, under pretty much any conditions. *Anything*. With yields six to eight times greater than you'd get with even the most fertile soil on Earth.' She swigged down her drink, threw the carton into the bin in the corner like she was shooting a hoop. 'And there are no side effects, nothing dangerous in the food, nothing that could harm the environment – nothing obvious anyway –'

Rose raised her eyebrows. 'But you're gonna check it out properly, yeah?'

'Yeah, yeah,' bubbled Adiel. 'But used in the right way, rationed out and strictly controlled, this stuff could revolutionise farming. Turn around the world's food shortage. It could —'

'Radical thinking,' she said pointedly. 'Fynn would approve.'

Adiel's face clouded just a little, but she nodded. 'The proof of what Fynn did… It's buried. Buried along with his fungus.' She paused, as if wrestling with some problem – or maybe her conscience. 'I'm going to do my best to make sure it stays buried. I have to.'

Rose remembered Adiel's words back in the common room, when the girl had thought she wasn't being overheard. 'For the greater good?'

'The last thing we need is any whiff of scandal, any excuse for the corporations and multinationals to jump in and take control.' Adiel's expression had grown fierce, but now her face softened. 'And with Fynn dead too, all that belongs to the past. Better it stays there than comes out and jeopardises the future.' She smiled. 'That mud could save millions of lives. It honestly could. So I'm going to say it was spewed up in that mysterious volcanic eruption and file a claim in the name of the African people.'

'Seriously?' Rose smiled properly. 'You can do that?'

Adiel smiled and lowered her voice. 'With all the admin generated by our little "natural" disaster here, it'll take our sponsors months to notice.'

'And by the time she's finished doing her tests and telling the world what's what,' said Basel, breezing into the room, 'the paperwork will all be sorted, nice and legal.'

'Hello, here's trouble,' said Rose, grinning up at him.

He took off his straw hat and chucked it on a chair. 'People been either taking from us or giving us handouts way too long,' he said. 'Now we're gonna coin it, big time.'

Rose nodded. 'So *this* sort of bio-piracy's OK, then?'

'When the stuff you're pirating's from, like, Jupiter, it don't count,' Basel reasoned. 'Whole world's gonna want a piece of this miracle mud, and they can pay for it.' He tapped his nose. 'Through this.'

'Pricing will be fair, Basel,' said Adiel patiently. 'This stuff can help starving people the world over.'

'Uh-huh,' said Basel. 'Starting here.'

Rose smiled. 'You'll be sticking around, then?'

'Course. And I'm gonna keep schooling myself up. Gonna need credibility. It's us against the fat cats, the big businesses.'

'We'll need to buy ourselves out of the agri-unit system and set up independently,' agreed Adiel. 'It's going to be a hell of a lot of hard work... but we'll get there.'

There were different ways to save the planet, Rose reflected. Short-term fixes and long-haul solutions. Looked like Adiel and Basel and the others were in this for the duration, maybe for their whole lives. That was cool.

But what did the future hold for her? she wondered.

* * *

Solomon wondered how long it would take Adiel to find his letter of resignation on the shambles of her desk.

He'd waited a couple of days before making it official, but his mind had been made up from the start. It was time to go home. Not to the city. To the old village. Gouronkah, his home.

It had been almost levelled by the tremors from the volcano. Its people needed help; Solomon had been giving aid in secret for too long. Now he was going to do things properly. His kids had urban citizenship. They could make up their minds whether they would follow him back to Gouronkah or forge their own lives in the city. He would support them as best he could in whatever they decided.

But right now he needed to do this.

How many people had died because he'd touched a golden panel? And yet how many people might now live in the future because of the chain of events he had set in motion?

The Doctor said that if he hadn't touched the plaque ahead of the Wurms, the whole world might have ended up a smoking cinder. But the only smoking cinders he had seen were those of Kanjuchi, and the men on the gate, the animals and birds... They had all died in consequence of what he had done.

Solomon knew you couldn't change what you'd done in the past. But if you wanted to, you could make amends.

No more compromises, no more standing awkwardly between two worlds, no more wasting time. Solomon walked out through the main gates and very nearly smiled to himself. It was time to do things right.

The Earth's solar system was dwindling on the monitors, and Faltato was sipping tea and yawning in equal measure. He had spent a dark day and night wondering just how he would cope with the lengthy journey back to his ship.

The tactic he'd hit on was to lord it over the battered Wurm as much as possible.

He waggled his teacup. 'I think I'd like another, Korr. When you're ready.'

'I am not your servant, leggy scum!' the Wurm raged.

'But you are very, *very* grateful, I hope,' said Faltato smoothly. 'I saved you. Carried you out of that volcano myself. Under your warrior code, you owe me your life and your loyalty.' He settled back in his seat. 'So just ambulate along and make the tea, hmm?'

Already he was losing himself in future plans. He would leave with the finest of those art treasures on board, enough to pay off his debts, impress his peers and wow the ladies. He might even fund an expedition to locate that last, lost Valnaxi ship and its hidden vault of masterpieces. Or maybe simply set himself up in a little antiques place on Hastus Minor…

Korr wriggled painfully past him on his way out towards the galley.

'Two sugars!' Faltato called after him.

* * *

Rose went out to join the Doctor beside the smelly but salvaged TARDIS, free of the mud mountain at last. Through a yellow-grey cloud of volcanic smoke, the African sun was starting to set behind the shattered peak of Mount Tarsus.

It was a beautiful sight – but the Doctor had eyes only for his police box.

'You gonna wash it, then?' Rose wondered. 'It's well mucky.'

He considered. 'There's an Oulion rocket-wash opening on Titan in 900 years' time. Pretty reasonable rates, as I recall.'

'And what about this place in 900 years' time?' she asked.

'Year 3000?' He grinned. 'Middle of Africa's third golden age.'

'So it's gonna be goodbye to the Third World, then?'

He nodded. 'With a little help from a fourth.'

Rose frowned. 'You don't normally like that. I mean, nicking alien technology and stuff –'

'Oh, it's only mud! Anyway, it's always going on – fact of life,' he said dismissively. 'Is it better that the Henry van Stattens of this world get their hands on it every time? Nah, let the little people have a go. Let them grow big. 'Cause their dreams are even bigger.'

He looked out at the sunset himself for a while. Then he opened the TARDIS doors and she walked into the welcoming sea-green coolness of the control room. The Doctor banged the doors shut behind them and was soon tugging away at the console's switches and levers.

'What about those two Valnaxi? You're just going to leave them here on Earth?'

'Africa's been their home longer than anywhere else.' She shivered. 'One of them looks like me, though…'

'Maybe more than just looks,' he said distantly. 'When they sifted through you for the template…'

'What?'

'Oh, I dunno…' He looked pensive for a moment. 'They get one chance, that's all. But I think they'll be OK.'

'You *hope*,' said Rose.

'What's wrong with travelling hopefully?' He gave her a beguiling grin. 'I've turned it into an art form…'

He threw the final switch and the TARDIS heaved itself into the time vortex, taking them on to new adventures.

On the edges of the desert, Male and Female sat in silent wonder, feeling the setting African sun on their skin.

'The sun feels good,' said Male.

'Free,' murmured Female. '*Free* feels good. Free of the ancient obligations. There is nothing we can do for our race now.'

Male agreed. 'They will survive in their disembodied state. Perhaps they can sense their way back to the home world. Then –'

'There is nothing we can do for our race now,' Female said again, 'so we must live for *ourselves*.' She looked down at her bare arms. The golden pigment was slowly darkening.

'But where shall we go?' whispered Male. 'How shall we live?'

'You know from Solomon's thoughts that the old settlements are quiet and small and ignored. We shall find such a settlement. Or we shall start our own. It does not matter.' She closed her new eyes, worn dizzy with seeing. 'So much to experience in these forms. So much to suck in through these senses.'

'Endure,' said Male suddenly. 'We must endure, find a way to make art that endures. That we must do for our race.'

She shook her head. 'We have endured long enough. It is time we learned the art of *living*.'

Female rose and offered Male her hand. He took it.

Acknowledgements

Thanks first and foremost, as always, to the urbane and unflappable Justin Richards, who never makes a drama out of a crisis, though often besieged by both. Special thanks also to Jill Cole, Helen Raynor, Lesley Levene, Jac Rayner, Philip Craggs, Kate Walsh, Jason Loborik, Mike Tucker and Linda Chapman.

About the Author

Stephen Cole used to edit magazines and books, and in the late 1990s looked after the BBC's range of *Doctor Who* novels, videos and audio adventures. Now he spends his time writing books for children of all ages.

Recent projects include *Thieves Like Us* (a spooky action-adventure novel for young adults) and its sequel, *The Aztec Code*; the ongoing fantasy series *Astrosaurs* for younger children; and the surreal school mystery series *One Weird Day at Freekham High*. He lives in front of a computer in Buckinghamshire, venturing out of his office now and then to find his wife, Jill, and young son, Tobey.

Also available from BBC Books

Aliens and Enemies

By Justin Richards

ISBN-10 0 563 48632 5

ISBN-13 978 0 563 48646 6

UK £7.99 US $12.99/$15.99 CDN

The Cybermen are back to terrorise time and space – but luckily the new Doctor, played by David Tennant, and Rose are back to stop them.

Picking up where Monsters and Villains left off, this fully illustrated guide documents the return of these metal menaces, as well as the Sycorax and other foes from the new series, plus first series terrors like the Gelth and the Reapers.

More classic baddies such as the dreaded Zarbi, Sutekh and the Robots of Death also make a welcome appearance.